PROTECTING ALABAMA'S KIDS

SEAL OF PROTECTION

SUSAN STOKER

BRINIQUE AND DAVISA POWERS huddled under the blanket fort they'd made in their room, keeping their voices low so their parents couldn't hear them.

"I don't like him," Davisa declared stubbornly.

"Me neither, but Mommy and Daddy say he was like we used to be," Brinique countered.

Davisa's lower lip quivered and crocodile tears welled up in her big brown eyes. The tears fell and left tracks down her chocolate-brown face. "What if they decide they like him better?"

Brinique gathered her little sister into her arms and rocked her back and forth. She'd been looking after her all their lives. Before they'd been taken out of their home, she'd had to protect Davisa from the mean men their real mother invited into the house.

They'd only been three and four, but surprisingly, Brinique remembered it quite well.

Christopher and Alabama Powers had fostered, then adopted them. Even though they told her that it wasn't her job to protect her sister anymore, Brinique couldn't just turn it off. Physically, there wasn't anything that would hurt them in their new life, but emotionally, Davisa sometimes still struggled.

Brinique wasn't sure what it was that Daddy Abe did, but it was something really important. He and his friends would go out into the world and keep bad guys from hurting others. He was a SEAL...not like the animal, but some kind of military soldier. Brinique didn't really understand it all, but she knew he had to be the bestest soldier ever. When he held her in his arms and told her how much he loved her, she felt safe, so anyone he went out to help had to feel the same way.

The two years since they'd been officially adopted had been wonderful. She was eight now, and in the second grade. Davisa was seven and in first grade. They were the oldest kids in their class, but they hadn't started school, or even ever been read to, until they'd been taken in by Christopher and Alabama, and then they repeated a grade so they could catch up.

Earlier that week, Mommy and Daddy had told them they were going to get a brother. It had been a surprise, even more so when they learned their new sibling was actually older than them. Brinique liked being the oldest, liked it even better when she and Davisa were the only kids in the house.

Tommy had been with them for four days now, and it was a tough adjustment. Brinique knew what her sister was feeling, because they'd talked about it the other night...and she felt exactly the same way.

Tommy was ten. He'd been taken away from his father because of some bad stuff the man was doing. The little boy was skinny with dark brown hair. He didn't have a lot of clothes with him when he came to live with them, but Alabama's friends quickly took care of that. Tommy didn't talk much to adults...but when Mommy and Daddy weren't around, he said plenty to Brinique and Davisa.

He told them that they were ugly. And stupid. And that if either of them ever came into his room, he'd "knock the shit out of them."

"Why'd Mommy and Daddy have to bring him here? This is *our* house. I don't like him. He's mean," Davisa sniffled.

Brinique opened her mouth to answer her sister when the blanket at the edge of the fort shifted. Daddy Abe peeked in. "Permission to enter?"

Not really wanting to talk to her dad, Brinique nodded anyway. It would be rude to say no, and Daddy was a stickler for being respectful, no matter what. She shifted to the side, giving him room to wiggle inside the small space with them. The blanket dropped behind him, leaving the trio sitting in the muted darkness of the fort.

Brinique sighed when Daddy Abe wrapped his large arms around both her and Davisa. He smelled good. Like soap and...Daddy. She wasn't ready to snuggle into him like she'd usually do, but she couldn't deny it felt good in his embrace.

"I know you guys are confused, but I'd like to tell you a story," Christopher "Abe" Powers told his daughters evenly.

Brinique liked her dad's stories, but if his serious tone and the look in his eyes were any indication, she had a feeling this one would be very different. Davisa nodded immediately, and finally Brinique also nodded, refusing to look up again at her daddy.

"There once was a little boy," Abe started. "He lived with his dad because his mommy died two years ago. After the mommy died, the dad was very sad. So sad, he stopped caring about anything. He loved his wife so much that he had a hard time getting up in the mornings. He didn't wash his clothes or the dishes and only sometimes remembered to go to the store to buy food. He didn't go to work, because he was simply too sad.

"The little boy was also sad, but had to go to school. He tried to take care of his dad and the house, but he was only your age, Brinique. Only a kid. One day, his dad told him to pack a bag, they were leaving the house. They couldn't afford to stay there anymore. The boy was confused and upset because he couldn't take any of his toys and only a few clothes.

"They lived in their car for a while. Sleeping there and finding food to eat in trash cans behind restaurants. Finally, they were able to move into a trailer, but the boy's daddy still didn't seem to care about anything but drinking and giving himself shots with weird-looking liquid he melted on a spoon. The daddy the boy once knew was gone, and in his place was a mean man who always yelled at him and told him that he wished the boy wasn't there.

"Other mean people came into the trailer, and the boy hid in his room, hungry, and scared someone would come in and hurt him. You see, the nasty people visiting the trailer had hurt him before. His daddy would take money from the mean men, and they'd come into his room and hurt him. This went on for months. Then one day, after a particularly bad night with the mean people, when the boy was at school, his teacher told the principal that the boy was hurt. The police came and took the boy away from the mean people and his dad."

Brinique had turned to look up at her daddy while he'd been speaking. The light was low, but she could see his face. He looked incredibly sad. She didn't want to feel sorry for the boy in the story, but she did. She remembered all too well how scared she'd been when mean people came into *her* old house and talked to her mommy. "Was his dad sad his son was hurt?"

"No, Pumpkin," Abe told his daughter sadly. "He didn't care at all. When the police said they were taking him away to jail, he didn't seem to care about his son. He signed the papers that day to give his son up. The boy went into the foster care system like you and your sister did. Unfortunately, the things the nasty people did to hurt him have made him angry and sad at the same time. He's built a shield around himself, to protect himself from being hurt again. He's scared and confused about everything that happened, and I think he doesn't want to risk caring about anything, or anyone, ever again."

"It's Tommy, isn't it?" Brinique asked her dad in a small voice.

He nodded solemnly and squeezed Brinique affectionately. "I know this isn't easy on you guys. He's hurting and he's scared. All I'm asking is for you to give him some time. Be the wonderful sisters I know you can be. Don't take the things he says personally. You know your mom and I love you. You're ours. We picked *you* out of all the kids we could have. Remember?"

Davisa nodded and shifted until she was sitting in her dad's lap. "Yeah, you pickeded us. You didn't care if we were purple or had green hair. You love us because of what's inside our skin."

"That's right, sweetie. Tommy might have white skin like me and Mommy, but that doesn't mean that we love you any less or him any more. He might be angry and mean now, but we know there's a wonderful little boy in there. The protective, loving boy is there inside him...we just have to give him some time to let him find his way out. Remember how scared you were when you came here?"

Brinique and Davisa nodded at the same time, their eyes big as they looked up at their daddy.

"Right. He's feeling the same thing. He's scared he's gonna get taken away from another house. He's probably scared the mean people will find him again. And I know he misses his mom and dad. So we just have to give him some time. If he gets too nasty to you, just walk away and come into your room, or find me or Mommy. Okay? This is your home too, and you deserve to feel safe here just as much as he does. It's not all right to be rude, and I've made it clear that he isn't to say or do mean things to you two, but I have a feeling sometimes he'll do it anyway. I love you girls. More than you'll ever know. You're my princesses. Mine and Mommy's. Now... it's late. The sooner you go to sleep, the sooner a new day will come. You want to sleep in your fort tonight?"

"We can?" Davisa asked incredulously, knowing their daddy didn't like them to sleep under the loosely held-up blankets. He'd told them it was a safety hazard...whatever that was.

"Yes, Pumpkin. For tonight, you can," Abe confirmed, kissing the top of her head lovingly.

Abe helped drag pillows and blankets onto the floor and into the small fort and Brinique hugged him when he leaned down to kiss her good night. "I'm sorry mean people hurt him, Daddy."

"Me too, baby. Me too. I love you. Sleep well."

Later, Brinique looked over at her sister. Davisa was sound asleep next to her, but Brinique couldn't sleep. She kept thinking about what her daddy said about Tommy.

He'd been hurt. She didn't know *how* he'd been hurt, but it had to have been bad. She and Davisa had each other when they'd been placed into Mommy and Daddy's house. It had been tough and they hadn't trusted them for a long time. But Tommy didn't have anyone to watch his back.

She scrunched her little eyes closed and sent a fervent wish up to the stars. "Tommy needs a friend. He needs someone to talk to. I had Davisa, but he doesn't have anyone. He needs someone who will protect him from mean people. It doesn't have to be a kid. It could be a cat or dog…or even an imaginary friend. I want to be his friend, but he doesn't like me. I want him to be happy. To like Mommy and Daddy. To like *us*. Please send someone so he stops hurting."

Feeling better, Brinique relaxed into her blankets. Long ago, she'd wished for someone to protect Davisa, and the policemen had showed up. She'd wished for a mommy and daddy, and Christopher and Alabama had taken them to their home. She'd wished to get Mrs. Noonkaster for her teacher this year, and that had happened too.

So she had no doubt that *this* wish would come true as well.

She fell asleep with a smile on her face. Secure in the knowledge that soon, Tommy would get a new friend.

SOMEWHERE IN THE WORLD, in a place humans didn't know existed, lived the creatures adults liked to call "imaginary friends." Some were in the shape of animals that humans knew and loved...dogs, cats, rabbits. Others took on the form of gnomes or fairies. Still others looked like children themselves.

But tonight, the creature that was assigned to Tommy after little Brinique's wish arrived at their long-lost community, was the ugliest troll-like creature that called the place home.

Gamjee knew he was always picked last for assignments. Most of the time that didn't bother him. He liked being by himself. Knew his misshapen head and furry body scared children more than it comforted them. He was only sent out when there was no other imaginary friend available, or in the most dire of cases.

When the light above his bed turned on, Gamjee sighed. He'd just closed his eyes and hated being taken away from a nice long nap. Sighing, he got out of bed and got dressed. He closed his eyes and, in seconds, had transported himself to their king's throne room.

"King Matuna," Gamjee said respectfully, nodding his head at the large being who looked like a genie from one of the human's fairy tales. His bottom half was nothing but smoke, and his top half was the torso of a large human male. His face looked like a human's, but he had a huge mane of hair that stuck out around his head and flowed down his back.

"Gamjee," his king boomed. "You are being sent to a place called California. Your assignment is Tommy. He's having trouble assimilating into his new home, and it's imperative that he do so. The future of the country he lives in is relying on you."

Gamjee sighed. He didn't want an important assignment. He wanted to be assigned to some little kid who was scared of the dark and needed a buddy until he got over it.

But...they were never told the humans' futures; if

King Matuna was telling him that this Tommy boy was meant for big things in his world, he had to be very important.

"Yes, Sir," Gamjee said respectfully.

"Not only is his life in danger, he's mean. And we both know that being a mean kid can morph into being a mean adult, and that is not acceptable. Understand?"

"Yes, Sir," Gamjee repeated. But inside, he was scowling. He was tired and still wanted his nap.

"Off with you then," the king said.

Gamjee nodded and closed his eyes to transport to meet Tommy. The sooner he completed his assignment, the sooner he could nap.

CHAPTER 2

"Oooh, what in the world is *that*?" Davisa exclaimed squatting down in front of the bushes in the yard of their house.

Brinique came over to where her sister was kneeling and held back the branches of the bushes. Looking back at them was a pair of big, black, unblinking eyes.

It looked kind of like one of those gnomes people put in their gardens, except it was way more weird-looking, and kind of creepy to boot.

"Let me see," Tommy ordered, pushing the two girls away, making them fall back on their butts. Ignoring the fact that he might've hurt them, and only feeling bad for a moment, he peered through the branches.

"Holy crap, is that thing ugly," Tommy said.

"Who're you calling ugly?"

Tommy blinked and stared at the weird little creature, who hadn't moved. He whipped his head around to glare at Brinique and Davisa. "What did you say?"

"We didn't say anything," Davisa protested.

"Yes you did. You said, 'Who're you calling ugly?'"

"Did not," Davisa argued, standing up and putting her hands on her hips.

"Then who did?"

"I did."

All three kids turned their heads back toward the bushes.

The creature sat there, blinking back at them.

"D-d-did you just talk?" Tommy asked, obviously shaken.

"Yup."

"Statues can't talk," Tommy retorted.

"Well, it's a good thing I'm not a statue then, isn't it?" the creature said, standing up and moseying out from the bushes

"Is this a joke?" Tommy asked, looking around the front yard as if expecting someone to jump out from behind a car with a camera yelling, "April Fools!"

"No joke," the creature said, sitting down on the grass. "I can talk. What's with *them*?" he asked, indicating Brinique and Davisa with a tilt of his head.

Brinique was still sitting on the ground where she'd landed after being pushed, and Davisa was standing next to her...both staring at the creature blankly, their mouths open in disbelief.

Tommy, feeling the need to be brave, sneered, "They're girls. They're weak."

The creature threw his head back and laughed and laughed.

Not liking that he was being laughed at, Tommy pulled back his leg to kick the thing—

His foot stopped in midair, right in front of the creature, as if caught in a large hand.

Still laughing, the ugly little creature said, "Kicking me would be rude, now wouldn't it? And I'm laughing because, one, I've known some pretty amazing women...who were way stronger than a lot of men."

"Let go!" Tommy whined, hopping on one foot, while the other remained frozen in midair.

"Say you're sorry for trying to kick me," the creature ordered.

"I'm sorry, I'm sorry!" Tommy said frantically.

His foot was released from whatever it was that

had been holding it up and he fell back on the ground next to Brinique.

"I think we had better get the introductions out of the way...don't you? My name is Gamjee," the creature said. "I'm a troll. I'm not here to hurt you, but rather to help you."

Brinique was the first to find her tongue. She crawled forward and said, "I'm Brinique. This is my sister, Davisa, and that's Tommy."

"It's nice to meet you. Have you got any food?" Gamjee asked, licking his chops.

"I haven't had the opportunity to eat human food in what seems like forever."

"What are you guys doing?"

The voice came from above, and all three children spun guiltily to see their mommy standing behind them.

"We're talking to Gamjee," Brinique said with a big smile.

"Gamjee, huh?" Alabama Powers asked, kneeling with an indulgent smile on her face.

"Yeah. He's a troll," Davisa told her mom excitedly.

"Wow, a troll? What's he look like?"

Brinique frowned at her mom. "What do you mean? He's right there, you can see for yourself."

Alabama barely even looked down where her daughter was pointing. "I just thought you might like to describe him to me."

Davisa smiled huge and began telling their mom what she wanted to know. "He's got a really big head and it's kinda oblong with a weird dent near the top. He's covered in brownish red fur and has a pointy nose and really red cheeks. He's short too. Like, really short."

"I'm not that short," Gamjee mumbled grumpily.

Davisa ignored him and kept talking. "His feet are big and he's got a belly out to here," she pantomimed a large belly, "and he's hungry!"

Alabama laughed and stood up. "Well, it sounds as if he doesn't miss many meals. I don't have any troll food, but I might be able to find a can of tuna. You want to see if he'll eat it?"

"Yes!" both girls said immediately.

"Gross! Tuna," Gamjee said, wrinkling his brow. "Why do humans think we like to eat fish that's been sitting in a can for who knows how long? I prefer junk food. But I'd try a nice fresh salmon if it was offered."

"He don't like tuna," Tommy told Alabama matter-of-factly.

"Doesn't, not don't. And...he doesn't?" Alabama asked. "What does he like?"

"Junk food."

Alabama smiled down at the boy. "Junk food is bad for humans *and* trolls. Sorry. What else?"

Tommy turned back to the troll. "She says it's bad for us. What else do you want?"

"Do you think I'm deaf, boy?" Gamjee asked. "I can hear her as well as you can. I'm sitting right here."

"But she can't hear *you*," Tommy said in confusion.

Gamjee shrugged. "That's because she thinks I'm your imaginary friend. It's the rare adult, and only on very special occasions, who can actually see one of King Matuna's creatures."

"King Matuna?" Davisa asked.

"Yeah. There are thousands of us. We're sent all over the world to protect, assist, comfort, and keep children company. When we've met our quota of children helped, we get to have our pick of assignments...helping the Easter Bunny, moving up to the North Pole to help Santa's elves, or becoming a dream maker."

"What a dream maker?" Davisa asked.

"Someone who gets to change nightmares to happy dreams," Gamjee said simply.

"As if you'd ever be someone's *good* dream," Tommy said nastily.

Gamjee stared at Tommy for a long moment, then said calmly, "Tell your mom that a glass of milk would be great for now. Later, she can get me some hotdogs and Oreos."

"Milk?" Tommy exclaimed. "Gross." But he turned to Alabama. "He said a glass of milk will do for now, later he wants Oreos and hotdogs."

"And maybe later she can also make me a peanut butter and jelly sandwich," Gamjee said. "I haven't had one of those in forever, and I'd do just about anything for one. Even dance an Irish jig."

"You can dance?" Davisa asked.

Gamjee put his hands on his hips and turned to her. "What? You think just because I'm short and fat that I can't dance? I'll have you know that I was the Irish dancing champion in seventeen sixty-two."

Tommy couldn't help it. He giggled at the thought of this roly-poly creature doing any kind of dance.

Tommy missed the tender look Alabama gave him. He didn't realize that it was the first time he'd smiled or giggled since he'd moved in.

He also didn't realize that the small glimpse of happiness he showed to Alabama was the first time in a long time he wasn't afraid or scared about what would happen to him.

"I'll go and get some milk for your little friend, and a snack for you guys too. Don't wander off. I'll be right back," Alabama told the kids, running her hand lovingly over Davisa's head.

All three children nodded absently, still staring at the truly strange sight of the troll in front of them.

"So...um... Where did you really come from?" Tommy ventured awkwardly, once Alabama had walked away.

"Assbucket, Maine," Gamjee said, licking his chops.

"Ooooh, you said a bad word!" Davisa told the troll, her eyebrows shooting upward in shock.

"Oh...er...yeah, sorry," Gamjee said remorsefully.

"Maine? That's all the way on the other side of the country," Tommy told the creature. "You couldn't have come from there. It's too far."

"Well, I didn't walk, silly," Gamjee said.

"Then how did you get here?" Tommy asked in confusion.

"I transported," the troll told him.

"I don't understand."

"Magic. I got here by magic. The same way you can hear and see me and adults can't. I told you that King Matuna is the ruler of our town. He hears all the prayers and wishes of children around the world and decides if one of us needs to be sent. I usually don't get picked. The last time I got to leave Assbucket was nineteen forty-two…no…forty-four," Gamjee said in a rush, not caring that he was throwing a lot of information at the children.

Tommy, Davisa, and Brinique simply stared at the troll in confusion, not saying a word.

"Are you daft? Why aren't any of you saying anything?" Gamjee asked. "You're staring at me as if I put a spell on you."

"What's daft?" Davisa whispered to Brinique.

"It means crazy," Gamjee told the little girl, then sighed. "All you need to know is that I'm here now. I won't be staying forever, but you're gonna need me. You can talk to me, but no one else can hear or understand what I'm saying. They also can't see me. If you promise not to kick me," he glared at Tommy before continuing, "I'll hang out for a while. Can you please ask your mom to bring me some good food— I'm partial to cookies and sweets. Got it?"

"Yes," Brinique breathed.

"Cool," Davisa said.

"She's not my mom," Tommy grouched, his hands crossed over his chest belligerently.

"Does it matter?" Gamjee asked in a nonchalant voice. "I mean, you're living here, she cooks you food, gives you a roof over your head and keeps you safe."

"She's not gonna kee—"

"Here we are." Alabama's voice interrupted whatever it was that Tommy was going to say. "A nice big glass of milk for your friend." She knelt and put a tray on the ground in front of the bushes where Gamjee was standing. "I also brought my three favorite kids some lemonade in case they were thirsty."

Davisa and Brinique squealed in happiness and bent to pick up two of the plastic cups of lemonade.

Alabama smiled. "You guys doing all right out here?"

"Why wouldn't we be?" Tommy scowled at Alabama. "We're not babies. We can take care of ourselves."

"I just worry about you," Alabama said in a calm voice, seemingly not upset in the least by Tommy's attitude.

"Worry about the babies, not me. I can take care of myself."

"I'm not a baby," Brinique said.

"Yeah, we're not babies," Davisa echoed.

"I know you're older, Tommy," Alabama told the boy, curling her arm around Davisa. "And you're used to taking care of yourself. I feel better knowing you're out here with the girls, helping keep an eye on them."

"Mommy, he's not eyeing us," Brinique protested. "He's been ignoring us and throwing rocks at us."

"What have I told you about tattling, sweetheart?" Alabama asked her oldest daughter in an even voice. "It's not a nice thing to do. And he might've been throwing rocks, but I saw you pick one up and throw it right back. Two wrongs don't make a right."

"Ha, gotcha there, little girl," Gamjee said, lifting his head from the glass of milk he'd been slurping noisily as he made sure he didn't miss even a drop.

"Shut up, Gamjee," Brinique countered angrily.

"So, how did you come up with a name like Gamjee?" Alabama asked, obviously trying to stave off a tantrum and through magic didn't see the little troll pick up the glass of milk and drink it.

"He told it to us," Davisa said.

"Well, it's a nice name," Alabama said, smiling as she stood. "Ten more minutes then it's time to come inside. I have a snack ready, then it's homework time."

The children and the troll watched Alabama make her way back to the house.

The kids didn't notice, but Gamjee was well aware that the woman sat at a table next to the large bay window overlooking the front yard. She didn't read the book sitting in front of her, but kept her eyes on her children playing. Making sure they were safe.

"So, what's the deal, Tommy? She seems like a nice woman to me. Believe me, I've known some really not-so-nice people in my five thousand and seventy-three years." Gamjee picked up the conversation he and Tommy were having before Alabama came outside.

"My mom died."

"I'm sorry," Gambee said, putting his hands behind him, his enormous belly jutting out in front of him. "I've never had a mother, so I don't really know what you're going through, but I had a really good friend in Assbucket for two thousand years. He was really popular and King Matuna always sent him off on missions. When he helped enough children, he retired, and I haven't seen him in at least a thousand years. He was one of my only friends, and I miss him. The last little girl he helped lost her family when a whole mountain full of snow fell on their house and killed everyone but her."

Tommy didn't answer, but he looked unsure for the first time.

Brinique sat cross-legged on the ground next to them and said in a low voice, "Me and Davisa's first mom wasn't nice. She used to hit us and lock us in our room."

"And she didn't care when the scary men came into our room," Davisa added, sitting really close to her sister.

Tommy whipped his head around and looked intensely at the two girls. "Scary men came into your room? Did they touch you too?"

"Once," Brinique said in a soft voice. "He put his hand under my shirt and told me I was pretty. But that was all he did." She didn't realize that Gamjee had inched closer to her, and had put his small hand on her shoulder in comfort.

"I don't 'member," Davisa said. "But Bri told me that a man grabbed my arm and held me while he tried to take my shirt off." Now Gamjee went over to her, and brushed his hand over the hair flowing down her back.

"What happened?" Tommy whispered, leaning

toward his sisters without seeming to realized what he was doing.

Brinique shrugged. "Our mom yelled at us to get away from her friends. We hid in our room until they left. It wasn't too much longer that the police came and got us and we came to live with our new mommy and Daddy Abe."

"How do you know they aren't going to do the same thing?" Tommy asked quietly.

"Daddy's a SEAL," Brinique said simply.

"A seal shifter? Cool!" Gamjee breathed. "I haven't met one of those in a long time."

"No, dummy, not a shifter," Tommy rebuked. "A Navy SEAL. But that doesn't mean he won't hurt you," Tommy insisted. "Any man or woman can hurt anyone. He might be nice now, but he'll change."

"Mommy was like us," Davisa said solemnly, shaking her head. "She told us once. *Her* mom used to lock her in a closet. She wasn't allowed to talk. She didn't get to eat much."

Brinique picked up her sister's story. "Only she didn't get to be adopted by a nice mommy. She was beaten and starved and her mommy said mean things to her every day until she was old. When she married Daddy Abe, she wanted to help kids like us who had mean mommies and daddies."

Everyone was quiet as Brinique's words sank in.

"Do you miss your mom? Your *real* mom?" Tommy asked softly in a voice that was barely over a whisper, and one that the sisters hadn't ever heard from him before.

"No," Brinique said immediately.

"Uh-uh. Do you?" Davisa asked back.

Tommy nodded. "Yeah, sometimes. And I miss the dad I knew when she was alive."

"I miss Erasto," Gamjee said from Brinique's side. "That was the name of my friend. He didn't care that I had fur covering my body or that my nose and ears are pointy and don't match. He always played with me and shared the food and presents he received after coming back from another successful job."

Silence fell over the group for a moment, until Alabama called out from the front door, breaking the solemn mood. "Come on, kids, time to come inside."

Tommy and the girls stood. He turned to Alabama and tried to look as sad and pathetic as possible...even squeezing out a tear as he pleaded, "Can Gamjee come inside and stay in my room with me?"

He could tell Alabama was thinking very hard on what to say. Remembering what Brinique and

Davisa had said about the woman, and how she too had a mean mom, he did something he hadn't done in years.

Asked nicely. "Please?"

"Okay," Alabama relented in a soft voice. "But I'm sure your little friend will probably get homesick after a while and will want to go home. He might even be lost. So when he decides he wants to go, you have to let him go without a word of complaint, all right?"

All three children nodded vigorously.

"He isn't lost. He's from Assbucket, Maine," Davisa volunteered as they walked toward the front door.

"Davisa Powers! Language!" Alabama admonished in a not-very-harsh voice.

"What? That's where he told us he was from!" the little girl protested.

"I don't care. We do not use that kind of language in this house. Apologize."

"I'm sorry, Mommy."

Tommy tensed, waiting for the berating to continue, and was surprised when Alabama merely leaned down and kissed the top of Davisa's head. "Thank you, sweetie. You're forgiven. Now, everyone go wash your hands before snack time."

The black ball of suffocating goo that had taken root inside him, ever since Tommy realized his father had taken money in return for letting the mean men go into his bedroom, shrank a size at Alabama's words.

She'd brushed off the fact that Davisa had done something she wasn't supposed to as if she honestly didn't care anymore. All it had taken was an apology, and she'd turned back into the nice woman he'd observed since he'd arrived.

Tommy had learned to live with the awful feeling of the black ball inside him for so long, he'd almost forgotten what it felt like to be free of it.

He followed Brinique and Davisa into the house so he could wash his hands, refusing to think about what it all meant.

Gamjee stared up at the woman standing in the front hallway of the house as the children wandered off to wash up. She pulled out her phone and pushed a button and brought it to her ear. Gamjee listened, unashamed that he was spying on the woman.

"Hi hon. No, everything's fine. I was just calling to let you know that your children have found an imaginary friend living in the bushes out front. ... Yeah, apparently he's a troll they named Gamjee. ... I don't know, but for now, I think it's okay. I think

Tommy was the one who started it. Maybe as a joke, but Brinique and Davisa are totally going with it. I can't bear to see them upset when Tommy informs them that their little friend left..."

Alabama continued to talk with her husband, the love and respect for the man easy to hear in her tone. Gamjee knew she couldn't hear him, but said anyway, "Don't worry, Alabama...when the time is right, your children will be ready to let me go. I got this."

Gamjee wasn't sure that he *did* have this, but King Matuna hadn't picked him for a mission in over seventy years. He wasn't going to let him down. Besides, every mission he successfully completed meant he was that much closer to possibly seeing his one and only friend, Erasto, again. He'd completed so many missions, he was allowed to retire and have his pick of assignments. He was currently Santa's right-hand elf, and loving every second of it...if the rumors he'd heard were true.

CHAPTER 3

"WAKE UP, TOMMY," Gamjee said, lightly smacking the little boy's cheek.

Tommy continued to whimper and thrash on the small bed.

Gamjee jostled the little boy's shoulder, trying to wake him up gradually so as not to completely freak him out.

"Wha? Where am I?" Tommy asked groggily.

"You're safe at Alabama and Abe's house," Gamjee told him. "Remember?"

Tommy groaned and turned onto his side and curled into a little ball, not speaking.

"What was your dream about?" the troll asked. "Once, Erasto had a doozy of a dream. Of course, when one of King Matuna's creatures has a bad dream, crazy things happen."

Tommy opened his eyes and asked, "Like what?"

"Let's see...there was that one time when all the light bulbs in my house exploded at the same time," Gamjee said evenly. "Or when Shengis woke up in his wolf form and his fur was green instead of its usual black."

Tommy sat up, wiping sleep from his eyes. "Did that really happen?"

"Of course," Gamjee told him.

"There's no such thing as werewolves."

"Just like there's no such thing as talking trolls?" Gamjee asked, rolling his eyes. "Look, kid. Just because you can't see something or haven't experienced something doesn't mean it doesn't exist or can't happen."

Tommy, still looking freaked from whatever dream he'd had, asked, "Can you tell me more about your world?"

"You mean Assbucket, Maine? It's your world too. It's in the United States, just like California is," Gamjee said, looking down at his way-too-long fingernails as if he didn't have a care in the world.

"You're not supposed to say that word," Tommy told him.

"Oh, sorry. Right. Anyway, okay, let's see…so you know about King Matuna, who is our ruler. Well, all the animals in our world have special abilities."

"Like talking?"

"Of course they can talk," Gamjee said impatiently, waving a hand in the air. "But that's not what I mean. Like Halasuwa has the ability to read the minds of the children she's sent to help, and Ekon can fly."

"Wow." Tommy's eyes were as wide as saucers. "So you're a troll, and there are werewolves and flying…whatevers. What else?"

Gamjee lay down on the bed and nudged Tommy until he too was lying back down. "Well, have I mentioned Roger the rabbit?"

"From the movie?" Tommy asked in awe.

"What movie? Gamjee asked, confused. "Roger's in a movie?"

"It's a cartoon," Tommy clarified.

"Then, no. The Roger I'm talking about is as real as you and me. He's six feet tall and is one of King Matuna's favorites. He not only can talk, but he can run faster than any of the cars in your world *and* he's bulletproof," Gamjee said.

"He sounds awesome," Tommy breathed. "How come he didn't get to come and see me?"

Gamjee frowned. He was well aware that he wasn't exactly the imaginary creature most children dreamed about, but he could hold his own...darn it. "Because," he said a little grumpier than he'd intended. Trying to change the subject, he added, "At least you didn't get Petunia."

"Who's petunia?" Tommy asked.

"Not who. What. She's a skunk."

"Like in Bambi?"

"In what?" Gamjee asked.

"Bambi. The movie. The skunk in your town is named after the one in the movie?"

"Of course not. Petunia was around way before any movie was made," the troll scoffed.

Tommy was confused for a second, but shook his head and came up on an elbow to continue his questions. "Does she smell?"

"Not unless she farts. She can clear a room with one little toot," Gamjee said.

Tommy chuckled, as the troll meant him to. There wasn't anything funnier than farts to little boys. "I'd like to live in your world," Tommy stated sleepily after he'd lain back down. "No scary men who can hurt me."

Gamjee knew there were plenty of things that happened in his world that were terrifying, like the debriefing every creature had to go through when they returned from their jobs. But the things humans could do to one another, and the things they could do to a child, were truly horrifying. He knew better than to tell Tommy any of *those* stories. He was living enough of his own horror story.

Gamjee spoke quietly. "It seems to me that you're in a safe place here, Tommy. Alabama and Abe seem nice."

"They won't keep me."

"Why not?" the troll asked.

Tommy shrugged. "None of the others did. No one wants an old kid like me. Not one who…was hurt. They want the little kids."

"Brinique and Davisa weren't little when they got here," Gamjee said, tilting his head and twitching his pointed little ears.

"Littler than me," Tommy insisted.

"You've had a crappy life so far," Gamjee said resolutely, "and it sounds to me like you need a break. And I have it on good authority that Alabama and Abe want to keep you."

"For now," Tommy said sadly. "Wait until I screw up."

"You planning on it?" the troll asked.

"No. But it always happens. I have a temper, and I can't control it."

"Oh well, just say you're sorry and it'll be forgiven. I screw up all the time and King Matuna always forgives me," Gamjee said matter-of-factly.

Tommy's voice began to slur as he slowly fell back to sleep. "I mish my mama."

Gamjee wasn't the most affectionate creature in Assbucket, but he did his best to comfort the little boy next to him.

"I miss my mom too," Gamjee said in a soft voice.

"I didn't think you had a mom?" Tommy mumbled.

"Then I miss *having* a mom," Gamjee insisted.

A soft snore came from Tommy after a few minutes had passed. Gamjee had used some of his special powers to help the little boy fall into a dreemless sleep.

Gamjee didn't need any sleep, none of King Matuna's creatures did when they were on the job. The troll lay on the bed, making sure Tommy felt safe even while asleep, and thought out loud. "I'm gonna have to keep a close eye on this one."

Healing Tommy was one thing. Keeping him safe from harm would be another challenge altogether.

* * *

"Christopher, I'm worried about Tommy," Alabama told her husband the next morning.

"I know, me too, sweet. But he's tough. He has me and you and his sisters. He'll pull through. Remember how hard it was to get Brinique and Davisa to trust us when they first got here? They spent a lot of time huddled together in their room hiding. You didn't think they'd ever come out and talk with us. It'll take some time. That's all." Abe pulled his wife into his arms. "Foster to adoption, especially with children as opposed to infants or toddlers, isn't easy. We knew that going in."

"I know, I know. I can't believe his own *dad* took money in exchange for letting those awful men do… well, you know."

Abe sighed and shut his eyes tightly. "I want so badly to get my hands on his father and kill him. I know the guys would have no problem backing me up. I bet if he ever gets out of jail, Tex could find him within seconds."

"But then I'd have to visit you while *you* were in prison," Alabama told him, wrapping her arms around his neck. "I like having you around too much to risk it."

"Ah, ye of little faith, wife. You know I wouldn't get caught if Wolf and the others had my back."

Alabama sighed and closed her eyes, resting her head on Abe's chest. "I just...I see so much of myself in Tommy, and I want to hold him tight and tell him that it'll be all right. He's just so hurt. I can't stand it."

"He'll get there. He's tough, Alabama. Exactly like you. Give him some time."

"I'm afraid if it doesn't work out here with us, he'll end up another statistic. I can't bear that, Christopher."

Abe continued to hold on to Alabama tightly. He didn't say anything, simply rocked her.

"If his father *does* ever get out of jail, and thinks he'll get him back, he'll have to go through me," Alabama said in a soft voice laced with steel. Her fingers clutched at Abe's shirt at his back as she fought against the angry feelings coursing through her body at the thought of Tommy being anywhere near his birth father.

Abe pulled back and put his hands on either side of his wife's neck, his large fingers caressing her nape as his thumbs gently pushed her chin up so she had no choice but to meet his gaze. "Wrong. He'll not get anywhere near you. He'll have to go through *me*. And Wolf. And Dude. And Benny. And Cookie.

And Mozart. And probably even Tex. And I could probably call up some Delta Force men I know, and they'd be happy to help out as well," Abe told his wife in a tone that held no doubt whatsoever.

"I love you, Christopher. Thank you for not thinking I'm insane for wanting to adopt kids who nobody wants."

"I love you too, sweet. And there *are* people who want them...us."

CHAPTER 4

FOR THE FIFTH day in a row, Tommy woke up after a full night's sleep. He didn't remember having any nightmares in the last week or so, which was a miracle, as he'd starting having them every night after being molested for the first time—and they hadn't quit until the weird little troll started sleeping in bed with him.

He somehow knew it was him. He had no idea how Gamjee was doing it, but he wasn't going to complain.

His life with Christopher and Alabama Powers was actually pretty...nice. He'd never had siblings, but he was starting to thawjust a little toward Brinique and Davisa. They kept out of his face and didn't steal his stuff, which was a step up from the last foster home he'd been in.

Everything was going so well...it made him nervous. Generally, when things started to go good in his life, it went to shit soon after.

"I'm hungry," Gamjee told Tommy as soon as he saw the boy was awake.

"You're always hungry," he told the troll without heat.

"True. What do you think is for breakfast?"

"Probably the same thing you had for breakfast yesterday, and the day before that and the day before that," Tommy told the overweight little man with a laugh.

"I keep hoping for bacon and pancakes," Gamjee groused.

Tommy rolled his eyes and climbed out of bed.

"It's Friday, right?" Gamjee asked, following Tommy into the hall and the bathroom.

"Yeah."

"And we're going to the beach this weekend."

The troll wasn't exactly asking, more reminding him.

Tommy sighed as he shut the bathroom door, closing him and Gamjee inside. He *had* forgotten about the upcoming trip. Alabama had told him about it earlier in the week. Saying that the group of men Christopher worked with had rented a ginormous house on the beach near the Naval base, and everyone—literally twenty men, women, and children—was going to spend the weekend hanging out together.

It sounded like a nightmare to him, but he knew he couldn't get out of it. It wasn't like Alabama was going to let him stay home alone.

"I guess."

"You guess?" Gamjee deadpanned. "You know what's at the beach, don't you?"

His mouth full of foamy toothpaste, Tommy asked, "No, what?"

"Seafood!"

Rolling his eyes, Tommy spit out the foam and rinsed his mouth. As much as he liked the ugly little troll, and loved that he could talk to him, he was starting to get a little annoying going on about food all the time. It was crazy that a troll no adult could hear could ever get annoying, but Gamjee had definitely started to push his buttons.

Feeling the anger that was always simmering under the surface of his skin start to bubble and hiss,

Tommy sneered, "I don't know why you care. Alabama and Abe can't see you or hear you. They don't care one whit about you or where you're from. It's not as if—"

"I'm from Assbucket, Maine," Gamjee interrupted.

Furious that the troll hadn't let him finish his thought, Tommy kicked out at him in frustration.

As had happened the last time he'd tried to kick the troll, Tommy's foot was stopped in midair. This time, however, it was also twisted, as if the invisible hand was turning it.

Tommy shifted his body into the twist to keep his leg from hurting and ended up facing the mirror. His hands were braced on the counter and he was slightly bent over. He huffed out in anger, frustration, and pain. "Let me go!"

"Are you going to kick me again?" Gamjee asked, completely unfazed as he climbed up onto the toilet seat and folded his arms over his chest.

"No!" the boy answered belligerently.

As soon as the word left his mouth, his leg was released from whatever force had gripped it. Tommy whirled around and finished his thought. "It's not as if anyone gives a crap about you. Even your precious king thinks you're a failure. You said it yourself, you haven't been sent to help anyone in years and years. You're fat, ugly, and stupid."

The black ball of goo inside him swelled up and filled his throat. Making him want to lash out and make the troll hurt as much as he did.

Gamjee regarded the little boy. "Is that what happened to you?"

Tommy felt the blood drain out of his face. "Shut up."

"You're not fat or ugly. And I don't think you're stupid, but maybe the other foster parents didn't really understand you."

"I said shut *up*," Tommy demanded, the blood rushing into his face in a wave of heat.

There was a knock on the door. Tommy wrenched it open, more than happy to get away from Gamjee. "What?"

"You're not supposed to say that," Brinique told her foster brother, obviously having overheard him tell the troll to shut up. "Mommy doesn't like it."

"I don't care, and *you* can shut up too," Tommy told her, brushing past her, making sure to knock against her when he did it. The little girl stumbled, and her shoulder hit the wall next to the door.

"Ow! Watch it!" she griped, glaring at him while she massaged her sore shoulder.

Tommy didn't even see the glare as he hurried down the hall to his room. He slammed the door as hard as he could, making sure Gamjee was still in the hallway when he did it.

But when he turned around, the troll was sitting on the side of his bed as if he'd been waiting there all along.

"Argh!" Tommy growled. "How'd you get in here?"

"Magic," Gamjee said with a smirk.

Tommy did his best to ignore the troll and stomped to his dresser. He pulled out a pair of jeans, which he hated—his last foster mother had bought them for him, and they were dorky, dark blue with silly lines on the pockets on the back—and a T-shirt he'd had since he was six. It was threadbare and too small, but Tommy didn't care. It was something from his "old" life. A life he hated, but missed at the same time.

He purposely didn't put on any of the clothes Alabama and Abe had gotten for him, wanting to rebel against them in any way he could.

"I haven't had seafood in years," Gamjee mused. "I'd love some lobster swimming in butter. Ooh, and some coconut shrimp, maybe some crab legs too."

"Jeez!" Tommy screamed, putting his hands over

his ears. "I used to think it was cool that you could talk. Now it's just annoying. I'm going to get some breakfast. I can't wait to go to school to get away from you!" And with that, Tommy stomped out of his room.

Gamjee grinned and closed his eyes to talk to his king. Matuna was always watching and listening, and always around if one of his creatures needed some guidance or reassurance. "That didn't take long."

"Nope. Getting him to *want* to go to school. Goal one, check," King Matuna agreed.

"The others won't be as easy."

Matuna sobered. "No, they won't. But this weekend, you can check the next two off."

"Yeah." Gamjee was silent for a moment, then asked, "Next week's when it's supposed to happen, right?"

"Right," King Matuna said. "He'll be ready."

"Are you sure?" Gamjee asked, nervously. "He hasn't been here that long. I'm not sure he's had a chance to really acclimate. If he doesn't bond with Alabama, Abe, Brinique, and Davisa, it's not going to work. He's not going to be ready."

"He'll be ready," his king repeated stubbornly.

Gamjee wasn't convinced, but nodded anyway.

"Go on, you don't want to miss breakfast," King Matuna told Gamjee.

Nodding, the troll hopped off the bed and closed his eyes, transporting himself to the kitchen to see if he could nab some of the delicious-smelling eggs Alabama was cooking for her children.

CHAPTER 5

"Now, I don't want you to feel overwhelmed, Tommy," Alabama told him from the front seat. They were in a mini-van headed down to the coast. Abe was driving, Alabama was sitting next to him, and their hands were clasped together over the center console between the two seats. Tommy wanted to roll his eyes, but the memory of his own parents doing the same thing when he was really young prevented him from saying or doing anything negative.

"There's going to be a lot of people there, but the house is huge. You'll have your own room, since you're the oldest boy.

"Great, a house full of babies," Tommy groused.

"Look at me, Tommy," Abe ordered, dividing his attention from the road in front of them to the rearview mirror.

Reluctantly, Tommy raised his eyes and met Abe's in the mirror. The man didn't often use that tone with him, but when he did, Tommy knew better than to disobey. He wasn't scared...exactly...but he didn't want to push his luck either.

"I know everything is new and you're unsure. That's okay. You're allowed to feel that way. But what you're *not* allowed to do is be disrespectful to Alabama or your sisters...or anyone else who will be there this weekend. Alabama told you that you'll have your own room, but what she *didn't* tell you is what she gave up to make sure you had that room to yourself. The room you'll be staying in is the one that *we* usually sleep in. Because it was important to Alabama that you feel safe and comfortable, we'll be sleeping on the pullout couch in the living room."

Tommy gasped and his eyes whipped to the woman in the front seat. She wasn't looking at him, but staring straight ahead at the scenery as it passed.

"Christopher," she said in a low, pleading voice. "Drop it."

"No, sweet. He needs to know," Abe returned.

Tommy saw him squeeze his wife's hand then his eyes came back to Tommy's in the mirror.

"Yes. We're sleeping on the couch in the living room and you have one of the master bedrooms to yourself. Alabama wanted to be sure that you could get away from the hustle and bustle of everyone if you needed to. Brinique and Davisa will share one of the rooms with bunk beds in it with Sara and John. They're four and three. The other couples there each have their own master bedrooms, and the babies will all be bunking in with them. So you're the only person this weekend who will have his own room."

Abe's voice gentled, but Tommy could tell he was still being very serious when he continued. "I get that you've had it tough lately, Bub. I wish to God that it hadn't happened. But it did. The only thing you can do from this point is go forward. As much as we all wish we could have do-overs, we can't. I wish I could erase it for you, but that's impossible. Alabama wishes she would've found you before you had to experience the other three foster homes, but she didn't. All I'm asking from you, while you're dealing with the shit that happened—"

"Christopher! Language."

Abe ignored Alabama's gentle admonishment and continued on as if she hadn't spoken, but

Tommy saw the corner of his lips curl up into a small grin before he did so.

"...is that you are respectful to Alabama and the other women and kids who are there this weekend. If you feel the need to let off some steam, or if you're confused or unsure about what's happening, you can come to me. Or any of my friends. We'll talk about it with you and help you understand what you're feeling, or we'll give you some space to work it out on your own. But respect is a hard line that me—and all the other men who will be there this weekend—will hold you to. Got it?"

"Yes, sir," Tommy said automatically.

"That's not what I meant," Abe told him. "I don't need or necessarily want you to call me that, unless you're comfortable with it. All our women have been to hell and back. If you really want to know their stories, we'll tell you, man to man, but that won't come without trust."

Tommy couldn't imagine what kinds of things Alabama and her friends had been through. They were all very pretty and had nice clothes; he'd seen pictures of them all over the house when Alabama had pointed them out. Abe had to be lying to him to get his cooperation.

"Deal, Bub?"

"Yeah, fine. Deal." Tommy was happy he was getting his own room, but he wasn't sure what to think about Alabama and Abe sleeping in the living room. It didn't seem like something Abe really wanted to do, and it was his experience that adults generally did whatever they wanted.

One of the men who used to come into his room used to tell him that if he did what the man wanted, and wasn't loud, that he'd bring him an extra sandwich afterwards. It was a give and take. Tommy wondered what Abe and Alabama would want from him in return. He was confused and uncertain, but knew to the marrow of his bones that Abe wasn't messing around with the respect thing.

"Anyway, as I was saying, sweetheart," Alabama continued, turning around in her seat to meet Tommy's eyes as if Abe hadn't interrupted her. "There will be a lot of people here this weekend. I wanted to make sure you knew about them all before you met them. Okay?"

"Okay," Tommy agreed, only half listening.

"All the men have nicknames. You know Christopher's nickname is Abe. Well, he calls his friends by their nicknames, and most of the women use their real names. It can be confusing, and at first it'll seem like there are twice as many people there, but you can call them whatever you want. All right?"

"Yeah." Tommy had wondered about that. Alabama called her husband Christopher, but Davisa and Brinique called him Abe, as did he.

"Good. So Wolf, or Matthew, is married to Caroline. Wolf is the leader of the group of soldiers Christopher works with. They don't have any children. Cookie, or Hunter, is married to Fiona. They also don't have any kids. Mozart, or Sam, is with Summer. They have a two-and-a-half-year-old girl named April. Then there's Dude, or Faulkner, and Cheyenne. They also have a girl, and her name is Taylor. Then lastly there's Benny, or Kason, and Jessyka. They have three kids, John, Sara, and Callie. They're four, three, and one and a half."

Alabama took a deep breath and continued. "It's okay if you don't remember all their names. I know it's a lot. Brinique and Davisa can help if you need it, but I promise that no one will get mad or upset if you don't remember."

"One more thing, Bub," Abe added, waiting for Tommy to acknowledge him. After the little boy nodded, he told him, "My friends will let a lot slide as far as the respect thing goes...but Dude will not. No, don't tense up," Abe quickly reassured Tommy, seeing him go ramrod straight in the seat. "He's not violent at all. He's not going to hurt you, but he's very protective of his wife and little girl. Cheyenne almost died having his baby, and he wasn't there when it happened. It still bothers him. He will not tolerate any kind of disrespect to Cheyenne or Taylor. Okay?"

Tommy nodded quickly, strangely glad for the warning. He couldn't always control his mouth, but he'd make an effort to do it around the man named Dude...and his family.

Liking that Abe was speaking to him as if they were equals, and not as if he were a baby, Tommy said softly, "Thanks for the warning."

Abe's lips tilted up into a full-fledged smile. "You're welcome, Bub. We've got another hour or so...you wanna watch something other than *The Little Mermaid*? Figure that's a little girly for you."

"Christopher!" Alabama protested. "There's nothing wrong with *The Little Mermaid*."

"You're right. There's not. For our little girls. But Bub seems like he'd appreciate something different. Right?"

"Yes." Tommy paused a moment, then added, "Please."

"See?"

"Whatever," Alabama huffed.

Abe was still grinning as he looked back into the mirror. "How about *Holes*? Have you seen it?"

Tommy shook his head. He hadn't exactly been in an environment where movies were watched the last couple of years.

"Good. It's awesome. We don't have enough time for you to watch the entire thing, but you can get a good start on it. Then if you want, we'll take the DVD player inside and you can watch it tonight when you go to bed. If that doesn't work out, you can finish it up on the way home. That sound good?"

"Yeah. Thanks."

Alabama got the movie started on the portable DVD player for him and handed him a headset. Before he put it over his ears, Alabama told him, "I'm really happy you're here with us, Tommy. Enjoy the movie."

Tommy knew she was serious. She wasn't just saying that. He could tell the difference. He'd had lots of grown-ups tell him lies like that in the last year or so, simply because it was expected of them. But they'd done it in front of people like the state workers or inspectors. But it was just them in the car. Alabama wasn't trying to impress anyone. Her daughters had headphones on and couldn't hear her.

He swallowed hard and put the headphones on quickly, wanting to drown out her words and the emotions they brought forth within him.

Alabama didn't know him. Didn't know how ugly he was, how broken inside. She wouldn't say that if she knew.

He tried really hard to tamp down the tears that threatened to break free. He hadn't felt wanted in so long, and her words nearly broke the brick wall he'd built up inside his chest to hold the world at bay.

The movie started and Tommy looked around the car. He could see Alabama and Abe talking together, still holding hands. Brinique and Davisa were engrossed in the mermaid movie, and Gamjee was snoring on the floor at his feet.

Tommy closed his eyes and pretended for just a moment that he was five again. That he was in the car with his real mom and dad and they were going on vacation, just like they used to. Before his mom died. Before his dad decided he loved drinking and his mean friends more than his son.

A hand wrapped around his ankle, and Tommy opened his eyes. Gamjee was looking up at him intently.

The music on the movie started, and Tommy brought his eyes up to it. He didn't want to think about talking trolls, about what had happened to him when he lived with his dad, or how he was just one wrong word away from being thrown out of one more family.

He lost himself in the movie, welcoming the numbness that settled over his heart.

CHAPTER 6

"GIVE IT HERE!" Tommy ordered Davisa with his hand out. They were standing on the spacious deck of the beach house with some of the other children.

"No!" she returned immediately, holding the last piece of watermelon close to her chest.

"You've already had two pieces. I've only had one. I want it!" Tommy yelled, advancing on the little girl.

"Mommy!" Davisa screeched, turning around and running into the kitchen.

The men were currently deep in discussion near the front of the house. The man called Wolf had gotten a phone call, and all of the men had gotten up to discuss whatever it was they needed to talk about away from the women and kids.

Davisa burst into the kitchen with Tommy right

on her heels. She ran behind Alabama and started to quickly gobble up the watermelon as fast as she could.

"Whoa! Careful now!" Alabama exclaimed, holding a plate full of fruit up and out of the way of the children. "What on earth is going on?"

"She's being greedy and won't share!" Tommy tattled immediately.

"That's not true! He didn't even want the last piece of watermelon until he saw me pick it up!" Davisa retorted.

Tommy glared at Davisa. "You're lying! You knew I was going to eat it. You just didn't want me to have it."

"Uh-uh!"

"Okay, let's all just calm down. There's plenty of other things you can snack on, Tommy. Look, here's a plate full of yummy fruit you can have first choice of." Alabama held out the large plate with melon, strawberries, raspberries, blackberries, and cherries.

"I don't want that crap. I wanted watermelon," Tommy said belligerently, his arms crossed across his chest.

"Otter-ellen," April mimicked as she came into the kitchen with Summer. At two and a half, she was currently in a phase where she liked to repeat things that people around her said.

"Did someone say watermelon?" Summer asked, hiking her daughter up on her hip.

"No. Because there's none left. Stupid Davisa ate the last piece," Tommy growled.

"Tommy, that's not nice. There's plenty of other things to eat," Alabama admonished gently.

"You're being greedy," Brinique said, entering the fray. She'd been outside playing, but had followed her sister inside after hearing the argument on the porch.

"Shut up," Tommy glowered at the other little girl. "You're not a part of this."

"Tommy!" Alabama said sharply, her eyebrows furrowing. "I told you when you first moved in that we don't use those words."

"Shut up, shut up, shut up, shut *up*!" Tommy yelled. "I hate it here! I hate *you*, I hate *them*; it's just all stupid! I'll say whatever I want, whenever I want! Shut up, shut up, shut—"

His words were cut off by a large hand covering his mouth at the same time Abe rushed past him to get to his wife.

Tommy struggled in the man's grasp, trying to get away.

"Calm down, Tommy," Dude said sharply from right behind him.

"Mumph," he murmured under the hand.

The large man behind him leaned down and said in his ear, "I said, calm down. Look at what your words did to her. *Look*."

Tommy raised his eyes to Alabama, not sure what Dude was talking about.

With one glance, he knew something was terribly wrong with the woman who had always been so nice to him.

Summer had managed to grab the tray of fruit before it hit the ground, and Alabama was on her knees in the middle of the kitchen, her arms wrapped around herself protectively, staring off into space. Abe had taken Alabama's shoulders in his hands. He'd turned her so she was facing him, and was crouched down trying to look into her eyes. She had a blank look on her ghost-white face, and Tommy could see Alabama's entire body shaking uncontrollably.

"Sweet, look at me," Abe ordered. "You're fine. You're here with me, safe and sound. Come back to me…"

Dude slowly removed his hand from over Tommy's mouth, but didn't let go of him. When

Tommy struggled again, the large man merely tightened his hold. He said in a low voice, "No. You'll stay right here and watch what careless words can do to someone. What *your* careless words did to one of the nicest women I know."

Alabama's hands came up and covered her ears. She began to rock in Abe's hold. "No, no, no, no."

"Shhhhhh, sweet...you're safe, she's not here. Open your eyes and look at me," Abe said gently.

"Dark. It's so dark!"

"No it's not. It's the middle of the day. Open your eyes, Alabama. See the sun. You're not in the closet. You're here with me, and our daughters and friends. You're safe, and she's not here. Trust me, sweet."

Alabama's eyes opened to a squint, although her hands stayed over her ears.

"That's it. God, I love your beautiful gray eyes. See? It's me, Christopher. You're fine. Come back to me now."

Slowly her hands fell from her ears and gripped his biceps, her knuckles white with the force of her hold on him. Her brows scrunched down in confusion. "Christopher?"

"Yeah, it's me. Come here." Abe wrapped his wife up, one hand going behind her head to bring it to the space between his neck and shoulder, and the other around her waist, pulling her into him. He swayed with her in his arms.

"Mommy?" Brinique said uncertainly.

"Come here you two," Abe told them, holding out the arm that had been around Alabama's waist. The other stayed right where it was on her head. Both Brinique and Davisa went to their parents, wrapping their little arms around Alabama and Abe as best they could. The four of them huddled there in the kitchen together.

After several moments, Dude slowly backed out of the kitchen with Tommy still in his arms, leaving the Powers family together. When they were in the living room, Dude finally freed Tommy.

The little boy backed away and stood there staring at the adults who were standing silently around him. The women looked concerned. The men looked unhappy. Tommy started shaking. He had no idea what had just happened—but he knew *he'd* done it.

"I didn't mean it," he said in a small voice that wavered. He shook his head quickly. "I just wanted the last piece of watermelon...I don't know what happened."

Fiona and Caroline took a step toward him, and Tommy backed up farther, until his back was against the wall. He was completely freaked out. What were all these adults going to do? Were they going to hurt him? Punish him? His breathing sped up.

The two women kneeled in front of him, not close enough to touch, but putting themselves at his eye level. "It's okay, Tommy. Don't freak. She's going to be fine," Caroline said softly.

"This happens sometimes. Abe will take care of her," Fiona soothed.

"But..." Tears came to his eyes, and Tommy impatiently wiped them away when they fell down his cheeks. "I don't know what happened," he repeated.

"I think we all need a timeout," Benny said easily. "It's nap time for my crew. Why don't we all just take a break. In a few hours, we'll get dinner started on the grill. That work for everyone?"

The men all nodded and the women gathered up their children and headed for their bedroom suites.

Tommy watched as everyone left the big living area except for Caroline. She stayed squatting in front of him. "I know you don't understand what happened, but I suggest that you go hang out in your room for a while. I'm sure Alabama will come and reassure you as soon as she can. Don't worry. You're fine, Alabama's fine, and Christopher is good too. You're not in trouble."

"How c-can you say that? I m-made her...you know," Tommy said in a wobbly voice.

"I do know. But *you* should know that neither Alabama nor Christopher will hold this against you. Everyone makes mistakes. You should ask Christopher about the huge mistake he made with Alabama once. She forgave him because she cared about him a great deal, just like she cares about you. Just take a break, Tommy. Relax, and I'm sure they'll talk to you about it later."

"Will Abe hurt me?"

"Oh, sweetie. No. I know you haven't been with them for long, but you are perfectly safe. They might be disappointed, but they will *not* hurt you. They took you into their house with the hope of keeping you forever." At the look of surprise that formed on his tear-stained face, Caroline nodded. "Yeah, forever. I'm not lying about that. They want a house full of children they can love. And they chose you. It's been years since they've taken in a foster child... why do you think that is?"

Tommy shrugged.

"Because they were waiting for *you*."

"Me?"

"Yeah, you. They could've taken in any number of children after they adopted Brinique and Davisa, but they wanted to wait for the child they knew in their heart was meant to be theirs. And that's you."

"But...I'm too old," Tommy protested.

"Too old for what?"

"To be adopted?" It came out as more of a question than a statement.

"Who said? The other families you'd been placed with? Jerk kids at school? Tommy, if you hear nothing else, hear this: They. Picked. You. They want to adopt you. You're *their* kid. And parents don't hurt their children. *Good* parents don't. And Christopher and Alabama Powers are some of the best parents out there. Just take a break. Hang out in your room and give them some time. Okay? Things will be fine at dinner. You'll see."

Tommy nodded, even though he wasn't sure he believed the pretty woman kneeling in front of him. He *was* happy to get away from everyone though.

"Go on, now."

Tommy sidled toward the hall and walked backward to the room he'd been assigned, not wanting to turn his back on the large great room. He vaguely noticed Gamjee following along beside him, seemingly unconcerned about what had just happened in the kitchen. When he got to the large bedroom suite, he quickly entered and shut the door once the troll had sauntered through.

"Woo-wee, young Tommy, you sure do know how to kill the mood," Gamjee drawled teasingly.

"I didn't know," Tommy said defensively.

The troll shrugged. "Well, you do now."

"What did I say?"

"Shut up. You said it several times, in fact. Alabama warned you that she didn't like those words, but you said them anyway."

"But…I didn't mean anything by it. I say it all the time. *Everybody* says it all the time. It's just words."

"Not to her, obviously," Gamjee said softly.

Tommy looked around the large room fearfully. "I gotta hide."

"What? Why?" the troll asked.

"Because Abe is gonna want to hurt me! He told me I had to be respectful and I wasn't," Tommy said, more to himself than actually answering Gamjee's question. He moved to the armchair in the room and got behind it. He pushed with all his strength until it moved. He shoved it up against the end of the bed. It didn't block the entire end, but it would have to do.

He straightened and looked around again. Seeing no other piece of furniture that he could move, he went to the dresser. Pulling the middle drawer until it fell off its track and onto the floor with a thud, he dragged it over to the bed. Tommy put it up against one side of the mattress, blocking off part of the access to the space underneath.

He went back and forth five more times, taking all of the drawers from the dresser over to the bed and stacking them up against the bedframe. When there was only a small space left, he grabbed two pillows and the bedspread from the top of the bed, and shoved them into the space under it. Then he pulled the sheet on the bed down, so it draped over the hole at the end of the bed that the chair didn't cover.

Finally, Tommy crawled underneath and stuffed the pillows into the gap he'd used to get under the bed, sealing himself into the large, now-dark space.

"What in the world are you doing?" Gamjee asked in a muffled voice from outside the safe space Tommy had made.

When there was no response, the troll repeated, "Tommy? What are you doing?"

"Hiding."

"I don't think your hiding spot is very good. Anyone who walks in will know exactly where you are."

"Yeah, but they can't get to me very easily. I'll know where they're coming at me from when they move one of the drawers," Tommy said matter-of-factly.

"Caroline said that Abe wasn't going to hurt you," Gamjee told him.

"Adults lie. He was really mad," Tommy's voice wobbled with both sadness and fright.

"I think you should believe her. Especially after what she said about them choosing you."

"No," Tommy said stubbornly.

Gamjee shook his head as if he couldn't understand, then jumped up on the bed and sat, his stubby legs dangling over the edge. "If you don't mind, I'm gonna hang out up here. The mattress is much more comfortable than the floor."

"Whatever," Tommy returned, clearly not convinced.

When sniffles started from beneath the bed, Gamjee sighed. He hadn't been around many human children, and he wasn't sure what to say or do to make Tommy feel better. He was good with bad guys and using magic, but not so good with inconsolable little boys. He was there to prevent what was going to happen soon from going bad...but this was a whole different thing.

Gamjee had a feeling if Erasto was here, he'd have figured out a way to make Tommy stop crying by now. But he wasn't pretty like Erasto. Children didn't feel the need to snuggle up to him to make themselves feel better.

Sighing, Gamjee sat quietly, swinging his legs back and forth as he waited for Tommy to stop crying.

CHAPTER 7

CAROLINE STUCK her head into Tommy's room later and told him dinner was ready.

"I'm not hungry," he told her.

"Doesn't matter. You need to come out and eat. Or at least apologize. Come on, I'll be right by your side. It'll be fine. You'll see."

Tommy crawled out reluctantly, missing the sad look Caroline gave him as he maneuvered around the drawers. He followed along behind her, his hands stuffed into his front pockets, head down, as they made their way to the large dining room. The table was piled high with grilled hotdogs, hamburgers, corn on the cob, more sliced watermelon, potatoes, and a plate full of chocolate brownies.

Some of the kids were milling around, and Dude,

Cheyenne, Alabama, and Abe were filling their plates with food.

Without waiting to be prompted, Tommy quickly blurted, "I'm sorry. I didn't mean to be rude."

Abe and Dude didn't look impressed, but Alabama and Cheyenne smiled at him.

"It's okay, Tommy," Alabama told him softly. "I'm sorry if I scared you with my reaction. Look, Christopher sliced more watermelon." She pointed to the platter piled high with the sweet treat and smiled openly, if a bit cautiously at him.

Looking at the juicy fruit made Tommy's stomach hurt, and not because of the black ball of goo this time. He merely shook his head. "It's okay. I'll just have a hotdog."

Chatter went on around him at dinner, and Tommy tried to control the butterflies in his belly. He knew he'd messed up, and had no idea what was going to happen later. He didn't think Abe was the kind of man to let what he'd done go. But he didn't know him well enough to know *what* he'd do to him.

After the dishes were done, everyone settled in the living room around the large television. Someone had put in a cartoon movie and most of the kids were avidly watching. The women were chatting softly amongst themselves. He'd noticed

Gamjee lurking around the table and snatching pieces of food Brinique and Davisa conveniently "dropped" for him.

"Come on, Bub," Abe said softly, putting his arm around his shoulders. "Let's go outside with the guys."

Tommy wasn't sure he *wanted* to go outside with Abe and his friends, but he nodded anyway and allowed himself to be steered out the door and onto the large porch, which overlooked the ocean.

Whatever was going to happen was going to happen now. Out on the porch, away from the women and other kids. Tommy was scared, but he straightened his spine and walked woodenly along-side Abe. He thought he was going to throw up, and if he did, the black goo would go spewing out, but he swallowed hard, trying to be brave.

Surprisingly, Gamjee tore himself away from Davisa and Brinique, who were still gleefully getting him whatever snack he wanted, and followed behind them.

Tommy thought to himself that it figured not only would he be punished, but the troll he'd thought was so cool because he could talk would witness it. He'd probably laugh his butt off later at him too.

Abe's friends kinda scared him. They were big and muscular, and Tommy could tell with just a look that they were ten times deadlier than the mean men his dad used to bring into the house. But the second he'd start to panic being around them, one of the babies or women would enter the room, and Tommy could literally see the men change in front of his eyes. Their hard gazes turned soft as they looked at their wives or kids.

But that had been before he'd talked back to Alabama. Before whatever had happened to her had happened. Now the men just looked angry...at him.

Abe led him over to a set of chairs and they both sat down. Tommy perched on the very edge of the chair, his fingers gripping the arms tightly as he waited for something to happen.

The other five men settled down into chairs in a semi-circle around them. No one spoke for a while, and the time let Tommy's imagination kick into overdrive. He knew there was no way he could fight all six men off. He'd once managed to hurt one of the men his dad had let into his room, but there would be no getting away from *these* men.

He looked around. There wasn't even anywhere he could hide. He could try to run, but Tommy had a feeling any one of the men would catch him quickly.

Even though they were old, they looked like they were in shape.

The cool breeze from the ocean brushed against Tommy's face, and he breathed in the salty air. He would've liked this, hanging out by the ocean, if he hadn't been freaked out and worried about what his punishment was going to be.

Just as he thought he'd completely lose it, Abe spoke.

"I thought we could all tell Tommy a bit about our wives," Abe said, sitting back into his chair as if he didn't have a care in the world. "He needs to understand a bit more about us. I think he believes our lives have been easy and smooth, and that we and our women can't really relate to anything he's been through."

Abe turned to look at Tommy. "What you've been through was bad. Make no mistake, Tommy, I am in no way belittling what happened to you, or trying to downplay it. Your trust was broken by the man who should've moved heaven and earth to protect you. I simply want to show you that even though life sometimes sucks, you can rise above it."

Tommy shifted uncomfortably in his chair. It wasn't what he thought Abe would say. He truly expected him to yell at him for talking back to

Alabama earlier, and tell him that he'd be leaving and returning to foster care the second they got back to the house.

He didn't want to talk about *anything* that had happened to him before he was taken away from his dad, with *any* of these men. He was broken and dirty, and if they didn't like him now, they *really* wouldn't like him after they found out about what had happened. Tommy also didn't want to know whatever it was they wanted to tell him. There was no way anything the happy-go-lucky women inside had been through could *ever* compare to what happened to *him*. No way.

"Listen, young Tommy," Gamjee said from next to him. "Don't judge. When you first saw me, you thought I was a statue and didn't know I could talk. I think you might be surprised by what these men have to say."

"Okay," Tommy muttered, keeping his eyes on the waves and not looking at the troll or the men around him.

Wolf didn't beat around the bush. "Caroline was blown up, kidnapped, stalked, beaten, knifed, thrown into the ocean to drown, and then finally shot at."

Tommy gasped and looked up at Wolf in shock. "She was?"

"Yes. But not *once* did she beg for her life. She simply continued to fight back, not giving up. She's the strongest woman I know, even if she doesn't think so. I've learned never to underestimate her."

"Fiona was kidnapped and sold to bad people so they could have sex with her," Cookie said bluntly. "I rescued her, but she still deals with what happened to her today. She gets scared if she sees someone who looks like one of her kidnappers."

Tommy couldn't breathe. He felt his breaths coming too fast, but didn't bother to try to control them. He felt Gamjee touch his calf, and surprisingly that small touch seemed to calm him and make him not feel quite so alone. He didn't look away from Cookie as he bit his lip, then asked, "They touched her when she didn't want them to?"

"Yes, Tommy. For a long time. Months. I didn't know she'd been taken, but the moment I found her, I was impressed with how tough she was."

"How is she dealing with it?" Tommy asked. He really, really wanted to know the answer. It was vital.

"She has me. And her friends. We love her and support her, and she knows she's safe with us. That we have her back. I won't lie, she was in bad shape for a while. She still remembers what happened, and when she has bad dreams, I hold her and let her talk about them. If she doesn't want to talk, I simply hold her and let her cry. I love her, Tommy. I'd do anything for that woman. Anything."

Tommy nodded, but before he could ask another question, Mozart spoke.

"I met Summer when she was working up in Big Bend Lake at a motel. She was a maid. I went home to work, but when I went back up the mountain to visit her, she was living in an outdoor closet with no electricity or running water. She was starving and frozen, but she didn't want any help from anyone. Even me."

"What happened?" Tommy asked, his eyes wide.

Mozart grinned. "I convinced her to accept my help." Then he got serious again. "But someone killed my sister when she was around your age, and that person kidnapped Summer to try to make me sad. Luckily I got to her in time, and she's okay now."

"What happened to *your* wife?" Tommy asked Benny, practically holding his breath.

The other man laughed. "Well, it's more what happened to *me*. Her ex bashed me on the head and took me deep into the trees in a park. Then he sent her a picture of my bleeding head and told her if she didn't meet with him, he'd kill me."

"Holy cow!" Tommy breathed.

"Yup. She came to *my* rescue."

"But...she's handicapped," the little boy protested. "How could *she* save *you*?"

The six men around him all chuckled. Benny smiled at Tommy and said, "Don't let *her* hear you say you think she's handicapped. Yes, she was born with one leg shorter than the other and she limps, but she's never let *anyone* tell her she can't do something. She's more capable than some of the people I've met in the military."

Tommy then turned to Dude...the scary man he definitely didn't want to make mad. He'd scared him earlier today when he'd put his hand over his mouth, but thinking back on it, Tommy had to admit that the big man hadn't hurt him. At no time was the hand on his face cruel, and he didn't shake him as he held him still. Tommy realized the second he'd met Dude earlier that Abe really didn't have to warn him about being respectful to this man or his wife and daughter. Tommy had read the dangerous vibes coming off him loud and clear.

"Cheyenne had a bomb strapped to her chest by bad guys, not once, but twice," Dude said succinctly and without embellishment. "Not only that, but when we went to New York for a conference, another member of the family decided to try to blow her up a third time."

"And you saved her?"

"I saved her," Dude confirmed. "Then she almost died having my child. Look, I know society tells boys that they need to be tough and strong and not give a shit about anything other than themselves, but I'll tell you straight up, I cried the first time I saw Taylor. Cried like a baby. She was so perfect, and I know how hard both she and Cheyenne fought to bring her safely into this world. I'll protect them both with my life. I'll protect them from anyone who says mean things, and I'll do whatever it takes to keep them happy for the rest of my life. I'm bigger and stronger than them, so it's up to me to make sure they're safe."

Tommy felt kind of grown up when these men swore around him. They were treating him as if he was an adult, not like a little boy. "What if your wife dies? Then what?" Tommy asked carefully. "You can't always be there to protect her. Maybe she'll get in an accident. Maybe someone will come in and shoot her when she's shopping. You can't be by her side all day, every day."

Tommy held his breath as the scary man eyed him. He honestly wasn't trying to be mean, wasn't trying to be a jerk. He knew firsthand that love couldn't always keep people safe. Look what happened to *his* dad after Mom died. He didn't care about anything after it happened. Not even his own son.

Dude leaned forward, putting his elbows on his knees and looking Tommy in the eye. "You're right. Shit happens. Abe has told us a little bit about what happened in your life. I don't know what kind of man your dad was...actually, no, I *do* know. He was weak. I'm not saying that to be a dick, Tommy. I'm saying that because it's the truth. You want to know what will happen to Taylor if Cheyenne is somehow killed? I would love that little girl even more, enough for both me *and* Shy. I'd continue to protect her the best I can. I would tell her every day how much I love her and how much her mother loved her. I'd never, *ever*, do anything that would hurt her. And, if for some reason I *did* do something stupid, she has five uncles who live right here in California, and one that lives on the other side of the country, who will step in to make sure she's safe. They'd kick my butt and make sure I got my act together when it comes to her." He paused a moment. Then asked, "Understand?"

Tommy nodded and ducked his head, fighting back his tears.

Abe spoke then, and Tommy was relieved he was ignoring the tears he was trying so hard to hold back. "Then there's Alabama, Brinique, and Davisa. It's time you heard their stories, Bub. I know you've heard a bit in passing, but you need to know the whole story. Alabama is gonna be upset that I'm telling you...not because she's ashamed of what happened, but because she thinks you're too young. But *I* know you can deal with this because of what you've already lived through in your life. I wish to Christ you *were* too young. I wish that you had nothing more to worry about than what toys you want for Christmas or what food you want to order at the fast food place we'll stop at on the way home tomorrow. But that ship has sailed. If you don't want to know, if you don't think you can handle it...tell me now, and I'll tell you only a few generic details."

Tommy looked around at the other men and swallowed hard, shoving the black ball down his throat. It meant a lot that Abe was treating him as though he was an adult. He probably didn't deserve it after what happened earlier, and Tommy somehow knew what Abe was going to tell him was going to be awful. But it would explain what happened with Alabama in the kitchen, and he needed to know all the details.

"I can handle it," Tommy told Abe softly.

Without any other word of warning, Abe started talking. "Brinique and Davisa lived with their mother, who was addicted to drugs...much like your dad was. Their story is so similar to yours, it's almost eerie. The only difference is that I don't think either of them really knew what love was. They didn't know their father, and their mom was always mean to them. They learned that the only people they could rely on was each other.

"Men started trying to touch them under their clothes, and their mom didn't do anything to stop them. Brinique guarded her sister from that as best a four-year-old could. Luckily, the police learned about their situation and got them out. They haven't seen their mother since that day...and I don't think they even care. Simply because they hadn't ever seen any kind of love from her."

"They didn't do more than...touch?" Tommy asked in a small voice. Brinique had mentioned the bad men the other week, but he wanted clarification.

"No. We don't think so. It's tough to get details

out of kids who are that young, but the doctor seems to think no one did anything worse."

Tommy swallowed hard against the lump in his throat. He'd heard Brinique say she'd been touched, but he was suddenly very glad that was all it had been for her. He wouldn't wish what had happened to him on anyone else. Ever. He nodded.

"So...Alabama. My wife grew up in a home where every day, she was belittled and treated like crap. She also didn't know her father. Her mother would lock her in a closet while she had parties to keep her out of the way. She only sometimes allowed her to have food. Not only that, her mom would hit her. Kick her. Smack her. Every time she opened her mouth, she was hit."

"But she got out and got adopted...right?" Tommy asked.

"No."

"No? I don't understand."

"When she was twelve, her mom hit her with a skillet. She was hurt so badly, the police finally got involved and she was put into foster care. Just like you were. Except no one wanted to keep her. She learned to keep her mouth shut while she was growing up, and even once she was away from her abusive mother, she was quiet. She didn't try to make friends, and just went through life living on the side, watching others." Abe paused and held Tommy's gaze.

Tommy looked back at the man who was being so honest with him. Who was treating him as if he were an equal. He didn't want to bring it up, but he had to. "What did I say today? What happened to her?"

Abe settled farther back on his chair and looked out over the dark ocean and sighed. "When she was growing up, while she was locked in that closet when she was as young as two, her mom would scream at her. Alabama would pound on the closet door, begging to be let out because she was scared and hungry, and her mom just yelled at her. Over and over, she heard the same words. Because they were said so many times, they became ingrained in her brain. Kinda like your name is. When someone says it, you naturally react. Understand?"

Tommy nodded. He had a feeling he knew what words Abe was talking about, but he kept his mouth shut, feeling sick inside.

"When we were dating, she told me about what happened to her when she was little, and I felt bad for her, but I didn't fully understand. Then I screwed up. Big time. So bad, that I thank God every day she gave me a second chance."

"What'd you do?" Tommy whispered.

Abe leaned forward in his chair, put his elbows on his knees and turned his head to look Tommy in the eyes. His words were flat and full of pain. "I told her to shut up."

The words echoed in the night, and Tommy inhaled sharply.

"When she needed me the most, I told her to shut up. She needed my support and love, and I didn't believe her, and told her to shut up when she was trying to explain what had happened. Those two little words brought back all the pain she had endured while growing up. It was as if I were her mom, telling her to shut up all over again. I almost lost her, Bub. It took me a long time to get her to trust me again. To get her to open back up to me and give me a second chance. I'm not sure I deserved it, but thank God she eventually forgave me.

"As I said, those two words make her feel like she's a little girl again. Powerless and scared out of her mind. When she hears those words, she feels every fist, every kick, every single time her mom used to hit her. *That's* why she doesn't like those words, and that's why she asked you not to say them.

"As far as I can tell, you yelling those words at her today brought back too many memories. She's been doing great. She's had therapy, she has no problem talking, she loves to chat with her friends. But lately she's been stressed because she wants you to feel safe. Alabama wants to protect you and keep you safe from anything that might harm you. Today was too much for her."

"I didn't mean anything by it," Tommy whispered, his eyes filling with tears and his lip quivering.

"I know you didn't. Just like I didn't really mean it when I said them to her years ago. But that doesn't mean the words didn't hurt her anyway," Abe said matter-of-factly.

Without a word, Tommy stood up and ran toward the sliding door. He fumbled with the latch before finally wrenching it open.

"Tommy, wait!" Abe ordered.

The boy ignored him and raced into the house. He stumbled into the living room and made a beeline for Alabama. She was sitting on the couch with little Taylor sound asleep in her arms.

Tommy threw himself onto his knees in front of her and buried his face in her lap. He wrapped his arms around her legs and sobbed. "I'm sorry! I didn't mean it! I swear. I'll never say it again! I promise!"

His entire body shook with his sobs and he hiccupped as he cried.

"What on earth...!" Alabama said in bewilderment. The men had followed Abe into the room, and Dude leaned over and took his daughter out of Alabama's arms.

Alabama put her hands on Tommy's back and caressed him. "Shhhh, it's okay, Tommy. It's okay. Calm down. Just breathe."

Alabama looked up in confusion at her husband. "What's going on?"

"I told him why his words hurt you."

"Oh, Christopher..." Alabama said sorrowfully.

"I know you didn't want him to know, but he needed to," Abe told his wife. "One, because I needed to protect you. I didn't want him to say it again. And two, because he needs to realize out of anyone in our house, *you* are the one who can most understand what he's going through."

Tommy kept his head buried in Alabama's lap as he cried.

"Come on, let's get him to his room," Abe said, putting his hand under Alabama's elbow to help her stand up.

She stood but Tommy didn't let go of her. Alabama leaned over and tugged Tommy up. He cooperated and jumped up into her arms. Alabama staggered under his weight, but Abe was there to steady her, and to help hold Tommy.

Tommy's hands snaked around Alabama's neck, and he buried his face into the space between her neck and shoulder. His ankles crossed at the small of her back and they headed out of the room toward the suite Tommy had been staying in. Brinique and Davisa quickly followed along behind their parents, not sure what was going on, but wanting to be near Abe and Alabama all the same.

Rounding out the procession was the small, ugly troll as the family disappeared down the hallway.

"Will they be all right?" Jessyka asked softly. Benny came up next to her and put his arm around her waist.

"Yeah."

"Did Abe tell him everything about Alabama and her kids?" Fiona asked.

"Yes. He needed to hear it. Especially after what happened when he told her to shut up this afternoon," Cookie said softly.

"They'll be fine," Caroline proclaimed.

"Yes, they will," Wolf agreed.

The group settled down with their kids, each lost in their own thoughts, as they prayed Abe and

Alabama would find the right words to make Tommy feel better. The boy hadn't had an easy life, and while none of them liked what had happened that afternoon, they all knew Alabama was tough, and so full of love that she'd already forgiven Tommy. Now he just had to open himself up to that love.

CHAPTER 8

ALL FIVE OF them lay in the large king-size bed. Tommy was between Alabama and Abe, Brinique was cuddled up to Abe's other side, just as Davisa was doing with Alabama. Gamjee had settled himself into a corner of the room…watching the humans.

"Why did my dad do that to me?" Tommy asked in a quiet voice, averting his eyes from Alabama's as he lay with his head on her shoulder. He could feel Abe along his back, could feel his even breathing. Tommy supposed he should've been scared about being in a bed with the large man, but he finally realized deep down that Abe wouldn't hurt him in any way.

"I don't know," Alabama said softly.

"I mean, we were happy! He loved my mom and me. I don't get why he'd change so much."

"Tommy, look at me," Abe ordered softly.

Tommy turned over onto his back, but kept hold of Alabama's hand as he did. He glanced up and saw Abe's intense eyes looking down into his.

"I don't know your father, but I believe that he loved his wife *and* you very much. Sometimes grief does weird things to people."

Tommy nodded sagely.

"It doesn't excuse him though," Abe said earnestly. "Not at all. I'm not condoning what he did to you in the least. Understand?"

Tommy nodded again.

"I have a dangerous job. Both Alabama and I know that every time I leave, I might not come home."

Brinique made a squeaking noise and buried her nose into Abe's shoulder.

"I'm not saying this to scare you guys," Abe hurried to reassure his family. "And I'm good at what I do. But just as there's a chance I might get hurt when I'm away, there could be an accident at home. Or a car wreck. Or someone could get sick. All I'm saying is that life is precious. I try to live every day as if it might be my last. That means telling Alabama that I love her every day. Making sure Brinique and Davisa...and now *you*, Tommy, are safe and happy. Because shit happens."

"Christopher," Alabama protested once more.

"Sorry, sweet." Abe smiled over at his wife apologetically. "*Stuff* happens. But I'll tell you what will *never* happen." He paused.

Tommy lifted his eyes and looked up at the large, imposing man next to him. "What?"

"If Alabama passed away, I'd never, ever do anything to hurt my children. I'd be sad, devastated, actually. I might get drunk a couple of nights with my friends. But I'm strong enough to know that you guys would be hurting just as much as I would. And you'd need me even more. And if I should die? And Alabama was left to raise you? She'd do the exact same thing."

Tommy's eyes wandered to Alabama. She was looking at Abe as if he'd just given her the sun and the moon. He recognized it because he used to see that same look in his mom's eyes before she died.

"To answer your question, Tommy," Abe went on. "I don't know why your father did what he did. But he was an idiot."

Tommy's eyebrows went up in surprise. "I don't understand."

Abe shifted until he had one hand free and ran it over the top of Tommy's head. "He had the best part of his wife right there next to him, and he couldn't see it."

"What's that?"

"You, Tommy. He had you."

Tommy's eyes welled up with tears again and he fought to hold them back. "I miss him. Not the smelly, scary man he was when I left, but the man he was before."

"I know."

"Our mommy didn't love us," Davisa said sadly from next to Alabama. "Why not? What did we do wrong?"

"Oh, honey," Alabama said sadly. "It wasn't you guys at all. Some people just aren't meant to be parents. Like my mom."

"Your mom was mean to you like ours was," Davisa said. It wasn't a question.

"Yes, she was. But that doesn't mean I wasn't loveable. Want to know how I know that?"

"Uh-huh."

"Because of your daddy. And you guys. And my friends in this house. Just because one person doesn't love you, doesn't mean you aren't loveable. It just means that other person is the one with the problem. Not you."

Davisa nodded and snuggled back into Alabama.

Suddenly, all three children giggled softly.

"What?" Abe asked.

"Gamjee is trying to pretend he's not crying," Tommy explained.

"Your imaginary friend, huh?" Abe asked, smiling. "Cool."

Eventually the children fell asleep, and Alabama looked over at Abe. "He's breaking my heart."

The big tough SEAL smiled. "You said the exact same thing the first week we had Brinique and Davisa."

Alabama smiled weakly. "It's as true now as it was then. Do you think he's gonna be all right?"

"Yeah," Abe told her immediately. "He's a smart kid. He's gonna work through this with our help. He's got that appointment next week with the child psychologist. She'll help him too."

"I love you. And for the record...you aren't allowed to die anytime soon."

Abe smiled over at his wife. "Same goes for you," he whispered.

They leaned over and awkwardly kissed each other over Tommy's prone body.

"Get some sleep, sweet. Things'll be better in the morning. I feel it."

* * *

SOMETIME IN THE NIGHT, Gamjee left the room and made his way into the big living room. Time was getting short, and he had to make a plan. This was a very sensitive subject, and King Matuna had told him it was imperative that Gamjee succeed. Tommy was meant for very important things in the future, and Gamjee was scared to death he'd screw things up.

He closed his eyes, and within seconds he could sense his king in his head.

"You think he's gonna understand when it happens?" Gamjee asked.

"I think he will, yes," King Matuna said. "After tonight, he has a better foundation and knows that Alabama and Abe want only the best for him."

"If he doesn't, this could end badly," Gamjee mused.

"He's got this. Have faith in him. And in yourself," Matuna semi-scolded.

"I'm worried that he hasn't had enough time to really understand and feel their love yet."

"He's had an awful life, there's no getting around that," King Matuna said. "But he's a smart kid. He knows a good thing when he sees it. And Abe did the right thing in telling him about the other women and about Alabama, Davisa, and Brinique. If nothing else, he'll do what he needs to in order to protect them. Besides...he has you."

For the first time in a really long time, Gamjee felt good about his job. Yeah, little Tommy *did* have him. He wasn't the biggest imaginary friend, and he wasn't the one most children would want, but when push came to shove, little Tommy had accepted him. He could've banished him back to Assbucket with just a thought, but he hadn't. He was still here, which meant Tommy wanted him here.

"I won't let you down," Gamjee told his king.

"I know you won't," Matuna said.

Gamjee nodded in agreement. "I'm ready."

One second his king was in his head, and the next Gamjee was alone once more. He crept back into the room with all the humans and stared at Tommy. The little boy was fast asleep, and for the first time since he'd arrived, Gamjee wasn't the one making him have good dreams.

"Sleep well, Tommy. It's gonna be a busy couple of days," the troll said in a low voice.

CHAPTER 9

SUNDAY MORNING at the beach house was uneventful. Well, as uneventful as a houseful of best friends and their young children could be. Tommy was quieter than usual as he took the time to observe all the couples together. Hearing what the women had been through had been an eye-opener. He'd been wallowing in his own head about what happened to him for so long, it almost made him feel better that there were others who had gone through similar experiences.

Not only gone through, but survived. It wasn't that he wished the awful things that had happened to him on anyone else, but seeing how happy Fiona seemed to be...as well as Brinique, Davisa, and

Alabama. It was…freeing almost. It gave him hope that he could one day be happy too.

The black blob was still there inside him, but it seemed smaller. It wasn't choking him anymore… not all the time like it had before.

On the way home, Tommy made a silent vow to try to be a better brother. A better kid in general. The end of the movie *Holes* made him realize something else…that what was meant to be, would be. Everything happened for a reason. Of course, in the beginning of the movie it was the boy being arrested for stealing shoes when he didn't do it. But everything that had happened to him afterward, no matter how awful it seemed to be as he was going through it, *had* to happen for him to get to a happy place. The message of the movie really hit home for Tommy.

When they got home, Tommy helped unpack the car, rather than stomping inside grouchily. He thanked Brinique when she handed him his suitcase. He helped Davisa carry the cooler back inside the house. And when Alabama asked him to water the plants, he did so without complaint.

Abe had noticed his new attitude and commented on it that night when he was saying good night. "I'm proud of you, Bub."

"For what?"

"For trying so hard. I appreciate it. You have no idea what it means to Alabama. And me."

Tommy shrugged. "I thought about everything you said this weekend. And...I'm sorry I've been so mean."

Abe put a hand on his shoulder. "I understand. I do. But you have a choice, and it's looking like you've already made it, and you'll never know how pleased I am by it. Everything you do in life is a choice. How you react to situations, what you say, what you do, how hard you try. You have every right to be upset and angry about what happened to you. But you also have the choice to try to put it behind you and move forward. You want to know the difference between a failure and a success?"

"What?" Tommy asked in a small voice. It had been a long time since he'd heard anyone say they were proud of him. It made him feel good. And made the black blob that had taken up residence in the pit of his stomach shrink to almost nothing. It was like it was now the size of a pea rather than a basketball.

"Not giving up and making the right choice," Abe told him, squeezing his shoulder gently. "Unfortunately, the right choice isn't always easy. And sometimes it's hard as hell...er...heck to figure out. But I know you're on the right track." Abe squeezed him affectionately and turned for the door. When he got there, he stopped and turned around.

"You should know, Tommy, Alabama and I want to adopt you. We want you as a part of our family permanently. We wouldn't have brought you into our home if we didn't want that. We don't care about the money the state gives us for fostering you. In fact, it's going into a bank account for *you* to use when you're an adult. But I thought you should know. I know it's fast, and the adoption won't happen for a while. But we would like nothing better than for you to be Tommy Powers. Remember that when you're making those choices. We aren't giving up on you—and we hope you won't give up on us either."

Then, without giving him a chance to respond, Abe closed the door behind him, leaving Tommy to his thoughts.

Monday and Tuesday, Tommy tried really hard to make better choices. It wasn't easy. Abe had warned him that it might not be, but he was trying. Tommy was still angry about what had happened to him. Still confused and upset about his dad. But the warm looks Alabama gave him when he said please and thank you went a long way toward soothing the beast inside him.

When Abe patted him on the back and said, "Thank you for looking after all the girls when I'm at work," it made him feel ten feet tall.

Not only that, but it was really hard to be grumpy around Gamjee. The troll was actually pretty funny. He let bad words slip more often than not, words Tommy knew if Alabama could hear, she'd be upset about. They talked nonstop about Assbucket, Maine, where the troll was from, and he told the funniest and most fantastical stories about what went on in their little town.

Tommy had asked where Assbucket was on a map, but Gamjee refused to say...telling him that if word got out about what a great town it was, everyone would want to move there and it would stop being such a wonderful place.

Gamjee had said that it wasn't a place humans could easily visit, but Tommy wished he could go there anyway. It sounded like there was a lot of craziness that went on...and he really wanted to see some of other imaginary friends children wished up.

"I wish you could go to school with me," Tommy told Gamjee one evening. "You'd make it so much more cool."

"School? No way," the troll sneered.

"But you could look through all the lunch boxes in the morning. Maybe even get some treats when the lunch ladies weren't looking," Tommy teased with a smile.

"Hmmmm, the lunch boxes have some appeal, but we know what goes on in school," Gamjee said. "Sitting still. No talking. Math. Reading. Noooooo thank you. I like staying here, hanging out until you get home."

"I have a question," Tommy said, sitting cross-legged on his bed, his elbows on his knees, his chin propped up in his hand.

"Shoot." Gamjee waved his hand, indicating for him to continue.

"How come me, Brinique, and Davisa are the only ones who can hear and see you? I mean, it would be really cool if the other kids, or even Abe and Alabama, could see you too."

Gamjee nodded and said, "Here's the thing. My kind usually doesn't interfere in the human world. It's kind of a rule. I mean, we visit and help make people feel better for a little while, but we never stay long and we never reveal ourselves to anyone but the one human we came to see. But I got special permission to let Brinique and Davisa see me too."

"Why?"

Why indeed. Knowing he couldn't say, Gamjee deflected. "Besides the fact I'm trying to earn my way to see my friend Erasto again. It's easier if they can see me. Look, you're a special little boy, and I wanted to make sure you knew what great people Abe and Alabama were. And the weather's better here in southern California than in Maine," he threw in with a laugh.

Tommy looked confused. "Why me, though?"

"Because you're destined to be a very special and important person in the human world, Tommy," Gamjee told him seriously.

"Me?" He shook his head. "I'm not important at all. You know what happened to me. I'm...dirty."

The troll didn't break eye contact with Tommy. "No. You're not. The men who hurt you are. I can't say what it is that you'll do in your life that will change the direction for all the humans in this country, but you have to believe me when I say you will. I'm here to make sure that you get that chance. To help you understand how special you really are."

"I don't understand," Tommy whispered.

"It's like the movie *Holes*," Gamjee tried to explain. "Everything you do has a consequence. You have no idea what you might be able to do for someone until perhaps years later. It's kinda like physics too. For every action, there's an equal and opposite reaction," Gamjee said.

"Huh?" Tommy replied, his forehead scrunched up in confusion.

"Newton's third law, you know," the troll said impatiently.

"Uh, nope. No clue."

"Shit, I forgot. You're only ten. That's not going to come around for another few years. Anyway, all I mean is that the things that happen today will have an impact on what happens years in the future."

Tommy nodded slowly. "You mean, like if I'm really mean and act like a jerk and Alabama and Abe decide not to keep me? That could mean something that might've happened to me in the future that's good, might not happen anymore?"

"Exactly." Gamjee beamed a weird troll smile at Tommy.

"So you're here because you want me to be good?"

Gamjee sighed. "Not exactly. Look, it doesn't matter. But you should know that I won't be here forever. In fact, I'll soon be going back to Assbucket. My time here is almost over."

"You're leaving? But...I don't want you to go...I like talking to you," Tommy pouted.

"I like it here too. Alabama is such a softie. And I've loved every single thing she's made for dinner. But, my place is in Assbucket, just like your place is here in Riverton with Alabama and Abe and your sisters."

Tommy stared at Gamjee. "My sisters?"

"Yeah, Brinique and Davisa."

"I hadn't thought of them like that," Tommy said.

"I have it on good authority that they think of *you* like that," Gamjee told him. "Just today, Brinique was bragging about you. She said that she had a new older brother."

"She was?"

"Yup. She told a boy in her class that if he didn't stop pulling her hair, her big brother was gonna beat him up."

Tommy looked at the troll in amazement as his words sank in. "I'm their older brother."

"Yeah..." The word was drawn out, as if Gamjee had said "duh."

"And I'm bigger than them. I can protect them if they need it. They haven't ever had an older brother before. Especially Brinique. She always had to protect Davisa, but no one was there to stand between her and her mom and the mean people."

"Nope," Gamjee agreed.

"And I have Abe to protect *me*."

"I think you're finally getting it," the troll said.

Tommy lay back on his bed and looked up at the ceiling, his mind whirling with everything the troll had said. But the thing that stuck out the most was— he was an older brother. He was *needed*.

He recalled what Dude had said. That it was his job to look after his wife and child because he was bigger and stronger than they were. He could do that for Brinique and Davisa. He could be their protector.

For the first time in forever, something clicked inside Tommy. Since his mom died, he'd felt lost. Thrown away. As if he was on his own. But suddenly, he wasn't anymore.

Tommy turned his head and looked at the troll, who was quietly staring back at him. "I'm gonna miss you."

"I'm gonona miss you too," Gamjee told him. "But you're gonna be busy growing up to be the important man you're destined to be. Maybe we'll see each other again one day."

Tommy nodded. "Someday I'm gonna get to

Assbucket. I wanna meet King Matuna and your friend Erasto."

"I'll look forward to it, young Tommy," Gamjee told him solemnly. "It will be an honor to have you there."

CHAPTER 10

WEDNESDAY HAD BEEN A GOOD DAY. Thursday, not so much. Tommy didn't like talking to the psychologist. Alabama had told him that there was nothing wrong with discussing what had happened to him, but every time he talked about it, the ball of black goo in his stomach grew and threatened to come up his throat and strangle him.

So he'd been grumpy at school before the meeting. He'd flunked a test because he didn't feel like taking it and had left it blank. He ignored his teacher when she told him to stop talking. He smacked a boy on the arm at recess when he wouldn't give him a ball. And he'd refused to talk to Alabama in the car on the way to the doctor's office.

The meeting itself was okay after all, though. The

woman he was supposed to talk to was nice and didn't force him to talk about anything he didn't want to, but Tommy was still on edge. Thinking about what the bad men had done to him, what his dad had *let* them do, was scary.

"I know it's hard talking about what happened to you, Tommy," the doctor had said in a soft voice. "And it might not ever get easier. But I promise that whatever you tell me in here will stay in here. This is a safe place for you."

"You won't tell Abe or Alabama?" Tommy asked. It was one of his biggest fears. He didn't *want* them to know exactly what had happened. He knew they'd probably understand, but it was too embarrassing, and he wanted them to see *him* when they looked at him, not what the men had done.

"No," the doctor reassured him. "What you want them to know will be up to you to tell them. But you can ask me anything you want about it. I'll always be honest with you. Even if it's hard to hear."

Tommy nodded, having new respect for the woman sitting in the chair in front of him. He hated being treated like a baby. "Maybe I'll have something to talk about next time," he conceded.

"Maybe you will," the doctor agreed with a smile.

He wasn't exactly in a good mood when they'd

left the doctor's office, but the black ball in his stomach had shrunk to a manageable size.

"You want to stop and get ice cream?" Alabama asked when they were on their way home.

Tommy shook his head. "No. It's okay."

"Are you sure?"

"Yeah. It wouldn't be fair if I got some and Brinique and Davisa didn't."

Alabama looked surprised at his answer, but she smiled hugely at him. "That's very thoughtful of you, Tommy. I'm sure they *would* be sad if they didn't get any, even though they didn't have to do the tough thing you did today. How about we all go out after dinner? You don't know this yet, but ice cream is one of Christopher's favorite desserts ever."

He smiled at Alabama. "Sounds good."

"I'm glad you're here, Tommy," Alabama told him.

"Me too." And he wasn't lying. Tommy didn't know how he'd lucked into getting Alabama and Abe Powers as foster parents, and maybe more—he wasn't ready to admit to that possibility yet, even after Abe had flat-out told him that they wanted to adopt him—but he wasn't going to complain about it. He knew a good thing when he saw it.

They pulled into the driveway of their house and Alabama told him, "Brinique and Davisa will be home soon. Caroline picked them up from school and will bring them home in about thirty minutes." She paused, then took a deep breath and continued, "I'm proud of you, Tommy. And I hope you don't feel bad about talking to someone. I still find it really useful sometimes. It's kinda nice to be able to talk to someone about how I'm feeling without having to worry that *they'll* feel bad about what I'm saying. I love Christopher with all that I am, but if I told him some of the stuff that's rolling around in my head, he'd want to fix it for me...and he'd treat me differently. And I don't want that. I want my husband to see me as strong and capable, even though I don't always feel that way...you know?"

"Yeah, I know," Tommy told her. And he did. He wanted to be normal, to be thought of as normal, but deep inside, he didn't really feel that way. The more he thought about it, the more he realized that Alabama was right. It might be nice to be able to talk to someone who didn't really know him. Who he wasn't living with all the time.

"Good. Let's go inside and get a snack. You can play in your room for a while and when Brinique and Davisa get home, you can all go outside and get some fresh air before it's homework time."

"Sounds good." Tommy climbed out of the car

and headed inside with Alabama. For the first time in a long time, he felt okay about his life.

Forty minutes later, Tommy was sitting on the steps leading up to the front door and watching his *sisters* play with Gamjee. They were playing a sort of keep-away game. Gamjee was keeping *himself* away from the little girls' grasping fingers. Tommy had no idea how he was doing it, as not only was he definitely overweight, but he had tiny legs that didn't seem as if they'd be able to move very fast, but somehow neither Brinique nor Davisa could manage to tag him.

"No fair!"

"You're cheating!"

"Catch me if you can!"

The happy voices rang out over the yard, and Tommy actually laughed at their antics. It had been a long time since he'd laughed at anything. At least it seemed like it.

He stood up to help his sisters and to join in the fun when a navy-blue car stopped in front of the house.

As if time switched to slow-motion, Tommy watched as his father climbed out of the driver's seat, leaving the door wide open, and stalked toward him.

He didn't understand how he could be there…he was supposed to be in jail.

Tommy backed away as fast as he could, stumbling over his feet and falling on his butt.

His father stood over him, hands on his hips, and glared. "Get up. Time to go home where you belong."

The big black ball in Tommy's stomach swelled up, cutting off his air and making it hard to breathe and impossible to speak. He shook his head. No, he didn't want to go with this man.

The father he once knew was gone. The man standing in front of him was skinny, much skinnier than even the last time he'd seen him. His hair hung limp and greasy around his ears and neck, and he even had a weird black tattoo on his arm where there hadn't been one before.

He reached down with a hand that Tommy noticed was streaked with dirt, with black stuff caked under his nails.

"I said get up," his father repeated.

"Leave him alone!" Brinique demanded. She'd come up beside him, and she was glaring at the man hovering over Tommy.

"Yeah! He's ours. You can't have him!"

Davisa's words felt good, but Tommy didn't have time to enjoy them. He scooted farther away from the man, knowing he was probably getting grass stains on his pants, but deciding Alabama would most likely forgive him once she heard how they got there.

Instead of continuing to reach for him, his father did something Tommy didn't expect.

He turned to Davisa and grabbed her by the upper arm, wrenching it upward until the little girl was standing on her tiptoes. She whimpered in pain even as she wiggled to try to escape his firm grasp.

"Fine. I'll take *her*. I know some men who'll love to get some black pussy."

Tommy didn't know what cats had to do with his sister, but whatever it was, it couldn't be good. "Leave her alone! I'll come with you!" He stood up quickly, trying to swallow the big black ball of goo, which had inched farther up his throat.

His father reached for Brinique instead. She tried to run, but wasn't fast enough.

"Forget it, I think I'd rather have these pretty young things instead. They're worth more money than you'd ever be," he said as he dragged the struggling and crying girls toward his car. Tommy ran after them, pulling on Davisa's free hand with all his strength. It didn't even slow his father down. He shoved Brinique into the driver's side of the car and snarled, "Crawl over, bitch, or I'll hurt your sister."

She immediately did as she was ordered.

Tommy saw how scared she was—and something twisted inside of him.

She was his sister. It was his job to protect her. The man who used to be his father might be bigger and stronger than he was, but Tommy knew first-hand what might happen to his sisters if they were taken away.

As Davisa was stuffed into the front seat along-side her sister, Tommy opened the back door of the car as fast as he could and jumped in. If his dad thought he'd take Brinique and Davisa and not him, he was crazy.

"Wait for me!"

Tommy turned right before he shut the door to see Gamjee running toward the car faster than he'd ever seen him move. He held the door open even as the car was moving away from the curb. The troll leaped into the open door and it slammed on its own as his father peeled away.

He saw Alabama fly out of the front door, screaming their names as the car sped off.

His father laughed maniacally. "I got me three little cash cows instead of just one. Fucking perfect!"

"That's a bad w-word," Davisa whispered from the front seat. She was huddled next to her sister. They both had their arms around each other and were shivering in fright.

Tommy thought fast. Over the last few days, Abe had told him a few stories about some of the situations he and his team had been in throughout the years. Including one where they knew they were outnumbered and wouldn't win by using force. They had to use their heads and fast-talk their way out of danger. Tommy didn't have any weapons, and the man who used to be his father was bigger and stronger than he was. He'd have to outsmart him.

He had no idea if he could, but if he didn't do something to try to help his sisters, he'd never be able to forgive himself. They were in trouble because of *his* birth father. Tommy was their protector, so he had to do what he could to make sure they were safe and his father didn't hurt them.

As if Gamjee could read his mind, the troll said, "Be smart, Tommy. Go easy. They're safe for now."

Nodding, but not looking down at the creature, Tommy leaned forward and lied like crazy. "It's about time you came and got me, Dad. I was waiting for you."

The man looked in the rearview mirror at his son

and narrowed his eyes. "That's not what I heard. And you certainly looked comfortable enough, lounging around the yard as if you didn't have anything better to do."

"I couldn't very well tell them I didn't want to be there," Tommy protested. "That didn't work so well in the other homes I was in. Besides, you were in jail. But I knew that you'd be coming for me as soon as you could. We're partners…right?"

Tommy inwardly winced at the phrase. His father had started saying that to him when he let the mean men into his room at night. He'd open the door, and Tommy knew what was going to happen. His dad would always be holding a bunch of money, and he'd look at him and say, "We're partners, Tommy. You do your part, and I'll do mine." Then he'd shut the door and leave him alone with the men who hurt him.

A wide smile formed on his father's face, showcasing the teeth that had once been white and pretty, and were now brown and broken. "That's right, boy. Partners."

"Do we really need them?" Tommy ventured to ask. "They're whiny little girls who can't keep their mouths shut. Let's just let them out on the next block. They're tattletales, and I thought it was just you and me…two peas in a pod."

He held his breath as his father considered his words. Tommy thought he'd convinced him, but his hopes were dashed when he said, "Naw. If nothing else, I'll just sell 'em. They'll be worth some good money for sure. I gotta get the hell outta this town. There was some mishap at the jail, and they let me out on a work detail. Dumb assholes. My stupid lawyer told me the names of your foster parents when I signed the papers saying I didn't want you anymore. It was easy enough to track 'em down. I took off and didn't look back, but I'm sure the guards will be looking for me by now."

Tommy thought fast and tried one more time to get his father to release Brinique and Davisa. "But the cops'll be looking for them. And their dad is one of those special soldier people."

"What do you mean?" his dad barked.

He tried to remember what they were called but he was so scared, he couldn't.

Just when he started to panic, Gamjee said, "SEALs, Tommy. They're SEALs."

"SEALs," he blurted out quickly. "In the Navy."

"Are you fucking kidding me?" He swore. "Dammit. That's all I need."

"Look, we can let them out here on the corner," Tommy suggested as they slowed to turn.

"No. No way. I need a hit. I can sell them tonight and leave town. No one will find me, it's fine. No one knows where I am. I'll just go into hiding. I can get some good shit with the money they'll bring in."

Tommy sat back in defeat. Tears welled up in his eyes. He'd failed his sisters the first time they'd needed him.

He didn't want his dad to sell the girls. Bad things would happen to them. He remembered the story about Fiona and how *she* was sold. A tear fell from his eye before he could stop it.

"Be strong," Gamjee said softly, so the girls couldn't hear him. "Wait for the right time. It'll come. You just have to have faith."

Tommy looked down at the troll. He was sitting on the floor behind the passenger seat. His belly was hanging over the belt of his pants and the hair on top of his misshapen head seemed to be sticking out more than usual. But his friend wasn't panicking, which helped Tommy keep control as well.

"I'm scared for them," he mouthed.

"Of course you are. They're your sisters. But right this second, Alabama is on the phone with Abe. They'll be here before you know it. In the meantime, you just have to stay calm and don't do anything rash."

Tommy nodded. He had no clue if what the troll was saying was true or not, but he had to believe it. Even if Alabama and Abe didn't care about *him*, they cared about Brinique and Davisa.

He wiped the tears off his face and took a deep breath. The black blob of goo was still there, but at least it wasn't choking him at the moment.

"You'll stay with me?" Tommy asked Gamjee quietly.

"Of course."

He nodded again then looked over at his sisters. Brinique was looking right at him. She had tears in her own eyes and her lip was quivering.

"It's okay," he mouthed to her. There was so much Tommy wanted to tell her, but now wasn't the time. He'd have to let his actions speak for him. His dad had hurt him, but there was no way he was going to let him hurt his sisters if he could help it.

* * *

"ALABAMA, CALM DOWN." Abe tried to soothe his wife. "Brinique and Davisa are wearing their necklaces."

"They haven't taken them off since they got them," Alabama agreed, as if he'd asked a question rather than simply stated a fact, breathless in her panic. "Have you called Tex yet? Is he tracking them?"

"Wolf is on the phone with him right now, and yes, he's got them. We're headed out the door. I've called Caroline and Fiona, they're on their way to you. The others have their kids, so for the moment we haven't told them what's going on. Let's keep it that way for now...okay? You can tell them all about it when our kids are safe at home."

"Okay. We need to figure out something to give Tommy that can be tracked. I don't think he's gonna want to wear a necklace."

"We will. I'm sure Tex is up to the challenge."

"How in the hell did Tommy's father get out of jail?" Alabama asked, now sounding pissed.

"I don't know, but right this second, it doesn't matter."

"You're right, sorry. I know you need to go, but Christopher...be careful."

"Sweet, I got this. I know you're freaked, but there is no way an asshole tweaker deadbeat of a father to *our* son is gonna get away with whatever the fuck he thinks he's trying to do. All right?"

She chuckled weakly, and for once didn't reprimand him for his language. "Well, when you put it *that* way..."

"I'll be home with our son and daughters before you know it. I really gotta go. The team's ready to head out. I love you."

"I love you too."

"Later."

"Bye, Christopher."

As soon as Abe hung up the phone, he turned to his teammates. "If he's touched one hair on any of my kids' heads, I'm gonna fuckin' kill him."

"And we'll let you. Come on, Tex sent the feed to our phones. Let's go get your kids back," Wolf said somewhat calmly.

To the casual observer, someone else might think his friend wasn't treating the situation with the urgency it deserved. But not Abe. He saw the ice-cold glint in the other man's eyes. He might sound laid-back, but he was anything but. No one fucked with one of their own. No one.

CHAPTER 11

TOMMY PACED the floor and tried to think about what he could do. His father had pulled up to a house Tommy had never seen before and hauled his sisters out of the car. He hadn't given them time to do anything but stumble along with him. He'd thrown them into a little bedroom and shoved Tommy in behind them. He'd then slammed and locked the door.

Not sure when he'd really started to think about Brinique and Davisa as his sisters, Tommy looked over at them. They had tracks on their brown cheeks where their tears had fallen and they looked extremely scared, but all in all, they were okay. His dad hadn't hurt them, which for the moment was the most important thing.

Their heads turned to the window when they heard a scratching sound. Tommy ran over, mad at himself that he hadn't noticed the window already. He pushed as hard as he could, but it would only open about six inches…not enough for either him or his sisters to get out. He was about to call Brinique over to help him push up on the frame when he saw the reason it wouldn't go any higher. There were nails in the wood of the frame, keeping it from opening all the way.

They were well and truly trapped.

Gamjee stuck his head in the narrow open space in the window, scaring the crap out of Tommy. He stumbled away from the window and glared at the troll.

"It'll be a tight fit, but I think I can make it," Gamjee told Tommy.

"I don't think so," Tommy told him, eyeing the small space and remembering how big the troll's stomach was.

"I *will*," Gamjee declared stubbornly. "Just watch!" He threw his body under the window and grunted in effort. Other than a large fart as he exerted effort to try to get though the space, nothing else happened. "Well, isn't this just a kick in the pants," he murmured, pulling away from the window with a frown.

One second the troll was standing outside the window, and the next he was on the bed behind the children, scowling.

Tommy looked from the bed, where Gamjee was, to the window. He turned back to the troll. "How'd you get in here?" he asked in confusion.

"Doesn't matter," Gamjee said. "What matters is getting you three out of here. Now, listen, Tommy. Your dad has—"

"He's *not* my dad," Tommy declared forcefully. "He might've been at one time, but I don't want anything to do with anyone who thinks it's okay to kidnap children—including his own flesh and blood —with the intent to sell them to bad people."

"Okay, then what do you want me to call him? What's his name?" Gamjee asked reasonably.

"I don't wanna use his real name. Not ever again! We'll call him…Herman. That sounds like a mean guy…right?" Tommy asked.

"Yup. That'll do. Okay, so Herman has left to go bring some people back to the house. We don't have a lot of time," the troll said. "How're we getting you guys out of here?"

"The window's out," Tommy said. "They nailed

it shut and breaking it would make too much noise." He went to the door to the room and pulled on the knob. It didn't even turn in his hand. "Locked."

"Is there anything we can use to knock it down?" Brinique asked, speaking up for the first time.

"Good idea," Tommy told her. "Help me look." He figured that if the girls were kept busy, maybe they wouldn't be as scared. It seemed to be working for *him*.

They looked under the bed, in the closet and in the couple of boxes that were strewn around the room. The only things they found were ratty, stinky clothes, a nest with baby mice in it, and some old broken dishes.

"What now?" Davisa asked, her eyes tearing up again. "I'm scared. I wanna go home."

Tommy bit his lip. He was scared too, but he was the oldest. He needed to protect his sisters. "We'll have to make a run for it," he declared. "There's three of us—"

Gamjee cleared his throat loudly.

"Sorry, there's three humans and a troll. When he comes back, we'll need a distraction." Tommy swallowed hard, not liking what he was going to say, but he instinctively knew it was the only way. "I'll mention my mom. Hopefully that will take him by surprise, then you guys can run away."

"But how will *you* escape?" Brinique asked in concern.

Tommy looked her in the eye. "You'll get help and bring them back."

"That's not fair," she protested weakly.

"He was *my* father," he said gritting his teeth. "Not yours. Besides, you're my sisters. It's my job to look after you."

Ignoring the look of disbelief that crossed her little face, Tommy turned to Gamjee. "I know you said that only we can see you, but maybe you can throw something between his feet? To trip him? I'll jump on top of him and give Brinique and Davisa more time to get away."

"What if he brings back lots of people?" Gamjee asked calmly. "What's the plan then?"

Tommy felt the black blob growing in his belly. He had no idea. He'd only been thinking about dealing with the man who used to be his dad. More men meant more people to hold on to his sisters so they couldn't get away.

He shook his head violently. "No. It doesn't matter." He turned to the girls. "As soon as the door opens, you two run. Your entire goal is to get outside. No matter what. Got it?"

"But what if you get hurt?"

"It doesn't matter. You get out and get help. And don't let go of Davisa's hand," he ordered Brinique. "I'll do what I can to help you. But promise me you won't stop."

"We promise, Tommy," Davisa said softly. She walked over to him and put her arms around him tightly. "We'll get help. We won't leave you here for long by yourself."

The black blob inside him shriveled a bit at her actions. He put his arms around Davisa's skinny body and hugged her back.

"Good. Now...Gamjee." Tommy turned back to the bed, but it was empty. "Where'd he go now?"

They once again searched the room, but didn't find hide nor hair of the troll. Brinique even asked the mice if they'd seen him, but they didn't answer her.

"Whatever," Tommy said decisively, feeling sad Gamjee had left them alone at a time like this. "He's a troll. A figment of our imagination. It's not like he could help us anyway. Here, Brinique, take a couple of plates. If you have to, throw them at the bad guys.

Davisa, you don't get any. Your only job is to hold on to Brinique. Okay?"

"Okay, Tommy."

He picked up a plate and a bowl and stacked the rest of the dishes near the door, just in case.

"Now we wait."

The girls nodded, and they all sat on the edge of the bed and listened for the man Tommy had dubbed Herman to get back.

* * *

WOLF, Abe, Cookie, Mozart, Dude, and Benny silently surrounded the decrepit house. The place was in a not-very-nice part of downtown San Diego. A part no cruise-loving or sun-seeking tourist would ever be caught dead in. The houses were rundown and the grass in the yards had been dead for quite a while. The few cars on the street were at least ten years old and most everything on them of value had long since been stolen for drug money.

The two blips on the apps on their phones had led them to a house that was one of the worst on the street. There were two rusted-out hulks of cars parked in the front yard, and the weeds were knee high. The concrete was cracked and broken in the driveway and sidewalk. The paint on the house had once been a nice yellow, but was peeling and broken now. The house was neglected and should've been condemned.

Abe gritted his teeth. His babies were inside that hellhole, and he wanted to burst inside and get them out. *Now.*

Knowing he was on the edge, but wouldn't agree to be anywhere than on the front entry team, Wolf had paired him with Dude. They all knew that Dude was the most deadly when it came to a child's life on the line. Almost losing his own child, then wife, had made him extra protective and pissed off when a woman or child was in danger.

Abe and Dude would make entry through the front door. At the same time, Benny and Mozart would enter through the back. Wolf and Cookie would take the front corners of the house to make sure no one busted out any of the windows, and to cover Abe and Dude's backs.

There had been three cars parked haphazardly around the house when they'd arrived. Including the same car Alabama had seen Tommy's shithead birth father peeling away in before she'd called the cavalry. Tommy's father's car was closest to the house, with the two others parked behind it.

Abe refused to think about what anyone in that house could do to three small, vulnerable kids—or how long they'd been in there.

He signaled to Wolf, who nodded back. It was time. Time to get his children back. God help anyone who got in his way.

CHAPTER 12

TOMMY, Brinique, and Davisa stood up when they heard the front door slam shut.

"This is it. You remember what to do, right?" Tommy asked in a voice he hoped was stronger than it sounded to his own ears.

"Yeah. Throw stuff and get out. Then get help and come back to get you," Brinique said in a shaky voice.

"That's right. Good. This'll work." Tommy tried to sound positive. "I know it will."

As soon as he finished talking, the door opened—and a man they'd never seen before stood there. He was wearing a pair of filthy jeans, sneakers, and a gray T-shirt with stains all over it. His face looked disgusting, covered in pockmarks, his hair was stringy and badly in need of washing, and his teeth were dark brown.

"Fuck yeah! Now this is worth paying two Benjamins for." The man grabbed his crotch and adjusted himself lewdly. He turned back to the other room. "I want both girls."

"No fucking way!" another voice complained. "You can't have 'em both. Fuck that shit. I get first crack at one."

"I don't give a shit what you guys do. I want the boy," a third voice drawled.

The man who'd opened the door backed into the other room, leaving the bedroom door open.

"Let's g-go," Tommy whispered. He knew exactly what the first two men were arguing about, and no way was he gonna let them get their filthy hands on Brinique or Davisa.

The three crept to the doorway and looked out. Two men were arguing with each other about who would get "first dibs" on the girls, and the third stranger was watching the argument while picking his teeth with a large knife. They were all tall and skinny, and even though they looked pale and sick, they were still bigger than Tommy was...and probably stronger.

Tommy's father was ignoring the men, fiddling

with a piece of rubber and trying to tie it around his arm. He'd seen his dad do that before, then give himself a shot in the arm with stuff he'd melted on a spoon.

The kids edged toward the door slowly, but as soon as they neared it, the guy with the knife said nonchalantly, "Your sweet pussy's about to get away."

The other two men whipped their heads around and stared right at them.

"Fuck. Get 'em!" one of them yelled.

Tommy pushed Brinique and Davisa toward the door at the same time, yelling, "*Go!*" He threw the bowl he'd been holding at the man closest to his sisters, somehow making a direct hit to his head.

The man stopped and threw a hand up to his now-bleeding forehead. "Fucker! That *hurt!*"

The second man who'd been arguing with the first almost grabbed Davisa's arm, but Brinique took the jagged piece of plate she'd been holding and thrust it into his chest as hard as she could.

Surprised that the young girl had fought back, he looked down at his bleeding chest in consternation, giving the girls just enough time to wrench open the door and bolt out.

"Don't let them get away!"

The two men ran out the door after Brinique and

Davisa, but Tommy didn't have time to worry about them, as the man with the knife *and* his father were both coming toward him.

Tommy threw the last two pieces of cheap china he had in his hands, but both men merely ducked. The plates broke harmlessly against the other wall of the small room.

"I knew you were lying about the whole partner thing, you little shit," his dad snarled. "Never were good for anything."

"You and Mom used to say that I was good at *everything*," Tommy shot back quickly.

"I lied," his father said, scowling.

"Enough of this shit," the other man growled. "Your ass is mine, kid." He held the sharp knife out in front of him—but had only taken one step before suddenly stopping.

Gamjee appeared out of thin air.

He stood in front of Tommy like a Viking of old. His thighs were as large as tree trunks, and in his hand he carried a huge mallet, which he held in front of him menacingly. He didn't exactly look completely human, but he didn't look a lot like the troll Tommy had first met either. He stood as tall as a wall between Tommy and the man with the knife.

"What the *fuck?*" the man gasped, gawking at the sight in front of him.

Tommy hadn't been sure the man could see Gamjee, but his harsh words answered that question. He wanted to stare at Gamjee as well—he looked as amazing as the superheroes in the comics he liked to read—but Tommy immediately started shifting sideways instead.

"Stay still, Tommy," Gamjee ordered in a deep tone he'd never used before. "I got this."

Tommy froze, scared out of his mind, but in awe of the troll he'd always thought was kinda weird.

There was nothing weird about him now. No jokes about food. No snarky comments about his size or smell.

"Gut him, Deke. Fucking freak," Tommy's father demanded coldly.

The man with the knife thrust it toward Gamjee —but the knife stopped in midair, just like Tommy's foot hhad when he'd tried to kick the troll.

He tried it again, with the same result.

"What the fuck?" he asked again, looking down at the knife in his hand, then at Gamjee. "Screw this!"

Tommy's eyes widened as the man pulled out a pistol.

"No, don't hurt him!" Tommy yelled.

But it was too late. The man emptied the clip at the small boy in front of him and the the larger-than-life troll who leaped in front of him.

"Door's opening," Dude said as the front door of the house slammed open right before they were about to make entry. Two little blurry streaks hurled themselves out of the house and straight into Abe's arms. He gathered them close and immediately twisted so his back was against the side of the house, out of the way.

It wasn't a moment too soon, because two men barreled out after the girls. The first was immediately taken out by Dude's powerful throat punch.

The second man fell over the first's motionless body as he followed close behind him. He looked up, saw Dude—dressed all in black and obviously pissed off—and bolted upward. He took off running but Dude didn't bother chasing, knowing his teammates wouldn't let him get away.

Abe watched as Wolf and Cookie shot after the man and took him down before he'd even run past the house next door.

Dude took a moment to look over at Abe,

Brinique, and Davisa. Abe nodded at him and gestured toward the now-open front door. It killed Abe that Tommy wasn't with his girls. This op wasn't over yet. Not by a long shot.

He crouched down and urged his kids to do the same. "Stay here," he said in a toneless voice to his children. "Right here. Do *not* move. Understand?"

Both girls nodded, the whites of their eyes bright in their dark faces.

Abe tried to tone down his "I want to kill the men who took you from me" voice. "You're safe. You did good, babies. I need to go and get your brother. Yeah?"

"Yeah. Okay," Brinique told him, her voice wavering, pushing at him with her tiny hands. "We're fine. Go get Tommy."

Just as Abe stood back up and nodded to Dude that he was ready to continue, shots rang out from inside the house.

Dude didn't hesitate. He took high point while Abe took low, and together they burst into the house, fingers on their triggers, ready to take out the threat to their SEAL family.

CHAPTER 13

TOMMY'S EYES widened when the bullets from the man's gun literally bounced off the giant troll and landed on the floor at his feet. One went wide and thunked into the wall, but Tommy didn't move from his position behind the wall of flesh in front of him.

"*What the fuck?*" the man shouted again, looking down at the gun at his hand.

"Freeze!"

"Put the gun down, asshole!"

"On the ground!"

"Hands up!"

The four voices sounded at the same time, and Tommy stood stock-still. Gamjee moved, and between one blink and the next, he went from the tall superhero back to the ugly little troll he knew so well.

Before Tommy could say a word, or even really understand what was happening, Abe was in front of him. "Are you all right? Are you hurt? Did you get shot?" His voice was hard and brusque, but not unkind.

"I'm okay!"

Abe's hands landed on his shoulders and he turned him around so his back was to the room. Tommy felt him running them over his back and legs. Then he was turned again, and then he was in Abe's arms, held tightly to his chest.

"Jesus! Thank God. Shit. When I heard the shots, I thought... *Damn.*" Abe's words trailed off.

Tommy could feel the man's heart beating hard against his chest, could hear his harsh breaths, and feel them against his skin. He wrapped his own arms around Abe's neck and buried his face into his strong shoulder.

Tommy had never thought that Abe would be that upset about *him* getting hurt. A thought struck him, and he jerked his head back. "Brinique and Davisa?"

"They're fine," Abe said without letting him go.

"Why aren't you with them?" Tommy asked.

Abe finally pulled back at that, still not letting go, but far enough so he could look into his eyes. "Because I know they're okay. *They* weren't the ones inside this house when shots were fired. *You* were."

"But they're yours. I'm not," Tommy said in a small voice.

"The fuck you're not," Abe returned immediately, wrapping his large hands around Tommy's face and holding him still so he had to look into his eyes. "You think I don't know that it was you who told my girls to run? You think I don't know you protected them from the man who was supposed to love and protect *you* for all your days? You think you're not mine in every way that matters after today? Bub, it's been a long time since I was as scared as I was a moment ago. It wasn't because of Brinique and Davisa. It was because *you* were in here. I was worried about *you.*"

Abe took a deep breath, and Tommy could tell he was trying to control a deeper emotion. "And if you tell your mother I said fuck, I'll deny it. I'm not doing a very good job, but I really *am* trying to curb the swearing thing." He tried to smile, but it came out more like a grimace. He took another deep breath and asked softly, "You're really okay? You weren't hit?"

Tommy shook his head. "No. Gamjee saved me."

It was obvious Abe didn't believe him, because he merely shook his head. "Bub, I don't care if you think your imaginary friend was here with you today. As a matter of fact, I don't care if magic sprinkles fall from the sky. I'm just glad as all get out that guy was a bad shot."

Tommy looked away from Abe then, and saw Gamjee staring at them. The troll winked at him and crossed his arms in front of his chest. Tommy thought the little troll's stance looked a lot like that of Abe and his friends when they did the same thing.

Abe stood up with Tommy in his arms and didn't waste a moment more before turning around and stalking out of the ramshackle house. His teammates were dealing with the drugged-out men inside, and Cookie and Wolf had the two who had chased after his daughters under control as well. Sirens were blaring in the distance as the police raced to their location, having been informed of where they were by Wolf right before they'd arrived, but Abe ignored them too. He put Tommy down and put his arm out to his daughters.

Brinique and Davisa ran toward their daddy and threw themselves at him, almost knocking him over. He picked them up, one in each arm, and the four of them went down the street toward Wolf's SUV. He opened the back hatch and sat both his girls down. Tommy crowded in next to Abe while he pulled out his cell phone.

He hit the contact that said "Home" and waited.

"Hello? Christopher?"

"Yeah. I've got them. They're all fine."

"Tommy too?" Alabama asked.

"Tommy too," Abe confirmed.

As Brinique and Davisa babbled to their mother, Tommy felt the black ball of goo, which had taken up all the space inside his belly since his dad had stopped being his dad and had started being a scary stranger, melt away. It simply disappeared as if it had never been there. Not even a pea-size blob was left.

Alabama had specifically asked about *him*. Not only her daughters.

Tommy had forgotten what it felt like to be wanted. To be loved.

Even though Tommy had only been with Abe and Alabama Powers for a short time, he knew a good thing when he saw it. He'd known it once before. And somehow, he knew his birth mom was watching him from heaven, and smiling.

Feeling something at his feet, Tommy looked down. Gamjee was standing there, and had taken hold of his pantleg. Tommy climbed out of the vehicle and kneeled down by the troll.

"Thank you."

"You're welcome."

"I'm sure Alabama will have the biggest cake you've ever seen waiting for us when we get home. I'll make sure you get some," Tommy told the troll, who he was beginning to think was the best friend he'd ever had.

"It's time for me to go," Gamjee said in a matter-of-fact voice. "I did what I came here to do."

Brinique and Davisa hopped off the back of the SUV and squatted down next to the little troll.

"No, we don't want you to go!" Davisa wailed, obviously still emotional from the last hour or so.

"Please, don't go," Brinique pleaded.

Tommy looked at the troll, then at his sisters. He felt good. Still shaky from everything that happened, but good. Different.

Suddenly, he knew what it was he wanted to do with his life. He wanted to protect others from bad men and women, like the ones who'd taken him and his sisters today. He wanted to do what Abe and his friends did, but not in the military.

He didn't know how, but he'd figure it out.

"Thank you," he told Gamjee again. "Someday,

I'm gonna get to Assbucket, Maine. I'm gonna meet King Matuna and your friend Erasto. I'm gonna sit down with you and have a nice meal and tell you all about my life, and the good things I've done with it. I swear I am."

"I believe you, Tommy. And I know you will, because my king has shown me the future. We'll meet again."

The little boy stood up and put his arm around Brinique, who had tears running down her cheeks. "It'll be okay, sis. He has places to go and people to help. Besides, I'm sure we can talk Mom into getting a pet when we get home. Right, Dad?"

Tommy could've sworn he saw tears in Abe's eyes, but if they were there, they'd disappeared when the large man blinked. "I think that can definitely be arranged...son."

Hours later, after eating junk food for dinner, after watching *The Little Mermaid* to try to get everyone back to normal, after speaking with each and every one of their friends and reassuring them that everyone was home and perfectly fine, after being reassured by the police that Tommy's dad would never be able to break out of jail again, after speaking with Tex and brainstorming ideas for a tracking device for Tommy, and long after the kids had gone to bed, Alabama and Abe lay naked and entwined in their king-size bed.

Neither said a word, just soaked up each other's soothing presence. Abe's hand moved from the small of Alabama's back down to her ass. He stroked up once, then back down. Alabama's hands moved as well. Caressing her husband's sides.

Eventually, he turned her so she was lying on her back. Abe moved down her body, using his lips and hands to show her how much he loved her. Lying between her legs, Abe pushed his hands under her ass and lifted her so he had better access to lick and suck at her sensitive nub.

Alabama writhed and arched her back as Abe feasted on her, making her explode in pleasure twice before he moved back up her body. He put the tip of his hard cock just inside her, then put both hands on either side of her face. He held her gaze as he slowly, very slowly, pushed all the way inside.

Still without words, speaking only with their eyes, Abe and Alabama made love. They celebrated the fact that their family was safe. Celebrated their bond, and celebrated their everlasting love.

Their lovemaking was tender and easy, and they both exploded together quickly.

Now sweaty and replete, Alabama and Abe Powers fell asleep, still as intimately connected as two lovers could be. Life may have thrown them curveballs, but together,r they'd learned they could conquer anything.

EPILOGUE

TWENTY-FOUR YEARS later

TOM POWERS WALKED toward a dingy diner in Assinippi, Maine. He had no clue if he was in the right place or not, the town was a dump and it looked like no one had lived there in generations. But a niggling voice in his head kept telling him to stop. To pull over and check it out.

Over the years, he'd visited dozens of towns in the state, looking for the one his troll long ago had called Assbucket, but which obviously hadn't really been called that.

The second he walked in, however, Tom knew he

was exactly where he needed to be. He'd found the town he'd spent years searching for.

From the outside, the town was a shithole. Decrepit buildings, unsavory-looking characters hanging around...but walking into the diner, it was as if he'd entered a different world.

The counter gleamed a bright white, the tops of the tables were pristine and clean, and not one of the leather bench seats was cracked. Several people smiled at him when he walked in and sat down. The air buzzed in a way he could only describe as magical, and he felt safe and content.

Yeah, he was definitely in the right place.

He was dressed in his usual work attire...black slacks, black suit coat, white dress shirt, and gray tie. In other towns he'd visited, more than one person had eyed him strangely, and several had asked if he was a "Man in Black."

He'd always smiled politely—it wasn't as if he hadn't heard that dig before—and continued on his way.

As he was sitting, his phone rang. Tom smiled as he answered. "Hey, baby."

"Hi. You find it this time?"

"Actually, yeah, I think so. I'll know more later. How're the kids?"

"Good. May misses you, and has already taped three videos for you about her days, for you to watch when you get home."

Tom's smile grew, thinking about his daughter. She was eight going on fourteen, and he thanked God every day for her. His wife hadn't had an easy pregnancy, and the doctor had warned that for the sake of her health, it should be the last and only child she birthed.

"And Chris?"

"Your son's as precocious as ever. He's into a 'green food' phase. He refuses to eat anything that isn't green. So it's been green beans, peas, lettuce, pickles, and I've used a lot of green food dye in things like milk and mashed potatoes."

Chuckling at that, Tom closed his eyes and rested his head on the back of the red vinyl seat behind him. He and Donna hadn't planned on having any other children after May. But Brinique had called him, worried sick about a child in her district who wasn't a good candidate for adoption. His sister worked for child protective services, and he couldn't be prouder of how she fought so hard for the children who didn't have anyone else to fight for them.

The child she'd called about had been diagnosed with Down syndrome and had been abused in his birth home. He was a ward of the state, and tender-hearted Brinique knew the boy would most likely spend his life in an institution if he wasn't adopted soon.

So he and Donna had gone to meet the child. And that was that. They'd started the paperwork that day to get approved to be foster parents, with the intent of eventually adopting him. Tom's father, Abe, was thrilled that they'd renamed the boy after him. Tom had watched his dad, the big bad retired Navy SEAL, cry when he'd held the one-year-old in his arms the first time he'd met him.

At four, Chris was now a handful, but he saw joy in everything and everyone around him. Tom couldn't imagine his life without him. "And you? How's my beautiful wife holding out?"

"I'm good, honey. You're coming home tomorrow, right?"

"Yes. I've been away from my family for too long."

"Well, you could always tell the president that he needs to stay home more," Donna teased.

Tom chuckled. "I'm not sure he'd go for that."

"I'm proud of you," Donna told him. "And not because you stepped in front of a bullet for him. I'm actually more *pissed* about that than proud," she said teasingly.

Tom didn't take offense. He knew quite well his wife's feelings about the time he'd seen someone pointing a gun at the President of the United States, who he'd been guarding—which was his job, as a Secret Service agent—and had stepped in front of the man, his Kevlar vest taking the bullet meant for the president. And he'd do it again in a heartbeat.

"I'm proud of you for the man you are. The man who sees people in need and wants to protect them. From the old ladies at the grocery store, to the kids you spend your weekends with at the Boys and Girls Club. From your own son and daughter, to your nieces and nephews. From me, to the President of the United States. No one is too big or small for you to step in to assist. I love that about you, and just plain love *you*."

"I love you too, sweetheart. I'll show you how much when I get home tomorrow."

"I'm counting on it. I went shopping today with your mom and her friends."

Tom chuckled. "I think it's kinda cool that you and my mother hang out so much."

"She's hysterical. And those friends of hers are pistols. I'm sure they keep their husbands on their toes."

Tom thought about his father's friends. Wolf,

Cookie, Mozart, Dude, and Benny. He wasn't sure he even knew their given names anymore. Their nicknames were all he'd ever called them by. But he'd never forget their wives. Their amazing, strong, kick-ass, beautiful wives.

"Oh, and Davisa and her brood are coming to visit next week, don't forget. It's spring break and she has the week off."

"I can't believe she's actually taking the week off," Tom mused. "Usually she uses the time when her students are on break to work on her classroom or do something else for the school."

Donna chuckled. "Looks like being an overachiever runs in the family. She loves those eighth graders. She was meant to be a science teacher."

"You ready to have all six of them descend on the house? I can still tell them they'll have to get a hotel," Tom told her seriously.

"It's fine. She and Lance will stay in the basement with Destiny and Jayden, since they're only two. Trinity and Malik will bunk down in May's room. And before you say it, yes, I know they'll giggle and talk and not get to bed until late every night, but May doesn't get to hang out with her cousins all that much."

"As long as you're okay with it, I'm okay with it," Tom told her.

"I hope you find him," Donna continued in a soft voice, changing the subject. "I know you've been looking for him for a long time."

She knew all about Gamjee. Tom had always known what he'd seen and heard when he was ten. His troll had morphed into some sort of badass bodyguard and stood in front of him, and somehow had made the bullets bounce right off his body. Every single shot, except for the one that hit the wall right next to Tom, would've torn through his body, and he wouldn't be here today if it wasn't for him.

Tom always remembered the conversation he'd had with the troll about how he had choices to make, and how one day he'd make a difference for everyone who lived in the country. He'd been right. If the president had died that fateful day, if he, Tom Powers, hadn't been there to take the bullet meant for the leader of the United States, there was no telling what would've happened. The vice president was weak, and wasn't respected by anyone inside or outside the country. If he'd taken power, things might be very different economically, politically, and even in Tom's own personal life.

"I'll find him when it's time," Tom told his wife

confidently. "I gotta go. Kiss the kids for me, and I'll talk to you tonight before I go to sleep."

"Okay. Love you. I'll talk to you later."

"Bye, honey."

"Bye."

Tom lifted his head from the seatback and clicked off the phone. He looked across the table in front of him—and smiled.

Sitting across from him was a little troll. And he looked exactly as he had the last time he'd seen him when he was ten.

"We meet again," Tom said with a smile, leaning his elbows on the table.

"Wanna blow this shithole of a diner and have a real meal?" Gamjee asked with a smirk.

"Only if it includes being able to talk with Erasto and King Matuna," Tom retorted.

"I think that can be arranged," Gamjee told him with a nod. Then he said, "Took ya long enough to get here. I was beginning to think you thought you were too good for me...saving the president and all."

"Not a chance. Assbucket isn't an easy place to find. I wanted to give you something to look forward to. Besides, I'm sure you were busy enough helping Santa out. You didn't miss me at all."

"Erasto's Santa's helper," Gamjee said. "I'm a

dream maker," the troll said proudly, his chest puffing out.

"Good for you," Tom said sincerely. "I still remember when you were with me for that week or so, I never slept so soundly or had such nice dreams."

Gamjee smiled. It was a crooked grin, and his ears and nose were still pointed and, honestly, the troll was still as ugly as ever, but Tommy couldn't care less. He'd learned over the years that it wasn't what someone looked like that made them a good person—or friend—it was what was in their hearts. And Gamjee was one of the best friends he'd ever had.

"I'm sorry Brinique and Davisa aren't here," Tommy said as they walked down the street.

"Their time will come. No worries," Gamjee told Tom. "Now…tell me about May and Chris. I want to know everything."

Not surprised the troll knew all about him and his family, Tom smiled as he followed his friend into a thick mist at the end of the street. He wasn't afraid. Not in the least. The troll had saved his life when he was ten. He trusted him with everything he had.

He couldn't wait to tell May more fairy tales about a town called Assbucket, and the magical creatures that inhabited it.

. . .

*

JOIN my Newsletter and find out about sales, free books, contests and new releases before anyone else!! Click HERE

Want to know when my books go on sale? Follow me on Bookbub HERE!
Would you like Susan's Book Protecting Caroline for FREE?
Click HERE

Also by Susan Stoker

SEAL of Protection Series
Protecting Caroline
Protecting Alabama
Protecting Fiona
Marrying Caroline (novella)
Protecting Summer
Protecting Cheyenne
Protecting Jessyka
Protecting Julie (novella)
Protecting Melody
Protecting the Future
Protecting Kiera (novella)
Protecting Alabama's Kids (novella)
Protecting Dakota

SEAL of Protection: Legacy Series
Securing Caite
Securing Brenae (novella) (April 2019)
Securing Sidney (May 2019)
Securing Piper (Sept 2019)
Securing Zoey (TBA)
Securing Avery (TBA)
Securing Kalee (TBA)

Delta Force Heroes Series

Rescuing Rayne

Rescuing Aimee (novella)

Rescuing Emily

Rescuing Harley

Marrying Emily

Rescuing Kassie

Rescuing Bryn

Rescuing Casey

Rescuing Sadie

Rescuing Wendy

Rescuing Mary

Rescuing Macie (April 2019)

Badge of Honor: Texas Heroes Series

Justice for Mackenzie

Justice for Mickie

Justice for Corrie

Justice for Laine (novella)

Shelter for Elizabeth

Justice for Boone

Shelter for Adeline

Shelter for Sophie

Justice for Erin

Justice for Milena

Shelter for Blythe

Justice for Hope
Shelter for Quinn (Feb 2019)
Shelter for Koren (July 2019)
Shelter for Penelope (Oct 2019)

Ace Security Series
Claiming Grace
Claiming Alexis
Claiming Bailey
Claiming Felicity
Claiming Sarah (Sept 2019)

Mountain Mercenaries Series
Defending Allye
Defending Chloe
Defending Morgan (Mar 2019)
Defending Harlow (June 2019)
Defending Everly (TBA)
Defending Zara (TBA)
Defending Raven (TBA)

Stand Alone
The Guardian Mist
Nature's Rift
A Princess for Cale
A Moment in Time- A Collection of Short Stories

Lambert's Lady

Special Operations Fan Fiction
http://www.AcesPress.com

Beyond Reality Series
Outback Hearts

Flaming Hearts

Frozen Hearts

Writing as Annie George:
Stepbrother Virgin (erotic novella)

ABOUT THE AUTHOR

New York Times, USA Today and *Wall Street Journal* Bestselling Author Susan Stoker has a heart as big as the state of Texas where she lives, but this all American girl has also spent the last fourteen years living in Missouri, California, Colorado, and Indiana. She's married to a retired Army man who now gets to follow *her* around the country.

She debuted her first series in 2014 and quickly followed that up with the SEAL of Protection Series, which solidified her love of writing and creating stories readers can get lost in.

If you enjoyed this book, or any book, please consider leaving a review. It's appreciated by authors more than you'll know.

www.stokeraces.com

susan@stokeraces.com

facebook.com/authorsusanstoker

twitter.com/Susan_Stoker

instagram.com/authorsusanstoker

goodreads.com/SusanStoker

bookbub.com/authors/susan-stoker

amazon.com/author/susanstoker

Printed in Great Britain
by Amazon